The Search

By G. K. Fralin

The Search

Second Edition

G.K.Fralin

ANT Publishing

Acknowledgements:

Victorine Lieske: Cover Image

Editing: Kristopher Miller and Joel
Fralin

Angela Cary: Epilog Image of Lunis
Flower

For my parents who taught me the source of love,

For my husband who taught me to embrace love

For my children who continue to teach me the endless capacity of love

Table of Contents

Author's Bio

G. K. Fralin lives in a small town of Wymore, Nebraska. She and her husband Joel have raised three children and have nine grandchildren. G. K. Fralin practiced as a practical nurse for 20 years and has since achieved a Bachelor's Degree in Business.

She now spends her time writing and enjoying her family. She has traveled throughout the United States, with no desire to leave her beloved Kansas and Nebraska roots.

"If you can't find material for drama, suspense, science fiction, spirituality, history, or romance here, you aren't looking." G. K. Fralin

Chapter 1: The Inn

Sheridan woke up alongside a country road where a thick late afternoon fog forced her off the highway the evening before. The unseasonable blinding whiteness was eerie, but not unheard of in Nebraska.

The mist took over so quickly the exit almost disappeared from view before she turned onto a Nebraska back road. She'd been headed to a book signing for her novel "Living Bedouin."

She wiped the sleep from her eyes. Every muscle stiff and sore, even with her slight five-foot-four inch frame, curling up in the back seat of her minivan made her feel cramped.

Peeling her sticky, thick tongue from the roof of her mouth made the icky taste even more like rotten food. She fished through her bag for a bottle of water. Finding it, she swished some around in her mouth then opened the window to spit into the heavy fog.

Reading the map, she determined she must be within thirty miles to Lincoln. The fog hadn't lifted. In fact, it was probably denser than the night before. She checked for a signal on her cell phone again, but she was in a dead zone and even the GPS wouldn't target a position. She would have to call Michael once back on Interstate 80.

She smiled at the thought of Michael. After three years of mourning the death of her husband, Mark, she was finally dating again. Michael had encouraged her to finish her doctorate in anthropology.

For over a month, Sheridan toured Nebraska, Kansas, Iowa, and Missouri promoting and doing book signings for her book based upon her doctoral thesis.

Along the way, she stopped in small towns and found church groups and other small town meetings. She set a goal of writing a book about the local communities, from the history of their founders, to the present day remnants of those roots.

The people were hospitable and their community strength often centered on church and family. The differences that seeped into their present day lives were their unique ancestral histories. With more research, most of which she could do from home, another book would soon be off to the publisher.

Sheridan loved her position with the university, and probably published enough to keep her on faculty. The idea of giving up the writing and particularly the research sickened her. Field research was the most fun.

The glaze of fixed concentration cleared from her mind and she could see the fog lifted. A few feet in front of her, an old, painted, wooden sign read Hidden 1/2 mile. The sign made her laugh, "Oh why not" she said aloud. It would probably take about a day to research one more town and it might put a nice ending to the new book.

First, Sheridan attempted a three-point turn on the narrow road to point her car back toward Interstate 80.

The fog bank became denser as she made the turn and felt her tires start to slide over the edge of a ditch. She managed to pull forward, safely back onto the road.

Shaking uncontrollably, Sheridan left the car to walk the half mile to Hidden.

Looking back toward the signpost, the fog had completely cleared. She looked behind her into an opaque white curtain. A shiver ran down her back as she walked the half mile into town. Looking back a few times the strange thick fog seemed to follow her. All landmarks disappeared one by one. She felt as if some sinister force was following her, pushing her toward Hidden.

A huge Victorian mansion greeted her immediately when stepping into the town. The huge double doors were wide enough for three or four men side by side to walk through.

A sign at the corner read simply 'Street'. She stood back and looked at it again trying to find the outline of faded letters or numbers in front of the word. There weren't any. There really wasn't room for anything but the word Street.

Stepping onto the wooden sidewalk in front of the building, she turned to look across to the other side of Street. *Oh, ho ho, this town is going to be very interesting.* She took a slow three-hundred-sixty-degree turn and saw it was the only visible street. She didn't see any alleys. However, footpaths broke up what she considered city blocks.

She looked down and noticed she stood in the middle of the street. *I must have twirled or something.*

Everything around her started spinning. There was a bench in front of the Victorian and she tottered toward it. As soon as she took her first step back toward the Inn, the dizziness was gone.

Okay, this is getting super weird. She threw the thought away deciding the dizziness was due to lack of decent sleep.

Sheridan turned her attention back toward the Inn.

From her vantage point in the middle of Street, she could see the long wings spreading from each side of the central section. The well-maintained, ancient building loomed imposing over the street.

Standing in front of the great walnut doors again, she noticed the left door had a large bronze knocker shaped like a flower that was obviously out of some artist's abstract mind. The other door boasted a matching bronze plaque, "Hide Inn: Come on In."

She ran her finger over the bronze flower and was shocked that it seemed softer than most bronzes. It was like bronzed baby shoes. She could feel the feathery shape of the petals and even striations of a feather. The grouping of petals was not unlike a lily. The abstract rendition reminded her of a painting she had in her living room of a rose bud in a vase that upon second look was a woman's hand.

The stem of the bronze flower made up the knocker and clanged like a heavy weight against its back-plate. Sheridan jumped in shock as she heard the noise reverberate through the interior of the great building.

As she waited, Sheridan looked across and down the street. All the buildings were limestone. Limestone quarries dotted the plains so it wasn't surprising. What did puzzle her was the buildings were all the same square design, except one.

The limestone across the street looked like a church of some kind. It had a sign standing in the yard with the words Angel Choir Chapel. The Chapel boasted a bell tower, but no visible doors

Why would anybody build a church with no front door? The curiosity of the researcher determined to discover the essence of the tiny town.

She suddenly realized there wasn't another soul visible. *So sad, another small Nebraska ghost town.* She sniffed the air. It was clean, like after a rain. No, it was cleaner. There were no farm smells, no alfalfa, animal feces, or fuel odors.

She slapped the back of her hand when she felt a sting and thought comically that they must have forgotten to take the insects.

A feeling of deep calm washed over her. She didn't know why, but she didn't want to question it. She almost felt drugged, like after taking a pain pill.

I really need some sleep before I fall over. She rubbed her arms and patted her cheeks. "Oh My." The words spread into a wide yawn.

She stretched her arms out and took a deep breath of the fresh air. The feeling of relaxation continued down her entire body as she inhaled the crispness deep into her lungs. She began to feel hazy and a little wobbly.

Then something else filled the air.

Sheridan felt goose bumps rise on her arms as she noticed a faint, melody. It had been there unnoticed since her arrival. It was like having the radio in her car on very low and suddenly noticing the music.

The sounds were the most beautiful harmony of voices she'd ever heard. It came from inside the chapel across the street. They sounded like a combination of halleluiahs, with an undertone of humming. Her heart lifted and warmth washed through her body. She wanted to go find the singer's but turned when she heard a movement behind her.

Methuselah opened the door of the Inn. The short, odd, little man looked like he bore the wisdom of the nearly 1000-year-old man from the Biblical comparison. Each crater-like wrinkle seemed to disappear when he smiled.

"Good morning young lady. Me thinks you have a problem with reading."

His gravely voice belied the youthful agility he displayed with a funny little jump and kick that reminded her of a leprechaun. He pointed to the sign on the door.

"I'm sorry sir, I couldn't resist the knocker. I've never seen anything like it."

"He's a curious flower, he is for sure." The old man's phrasing was so quaint she would have to make note of it to use in her book. He would make an interesting figure.

His face furrowed with deep wrinkles. His thick, wavy, gray hair nicely trimmed with a full, well-groomed beard. The man was somewhat stooped, but she noticed he stood erect very easily.

She enjoyed his theatrics, but wondered just how much she could trust the old guy. She tried to gauge his height compared by her own. She guessed him to be a few inches taller.

The odd, little innkeeper didn't fit the majestic feel of the Inn.

"Well I can see you are going to be an interesting guest."

"Excuse me?"

As he motioned her through the door, he enlightened her. "I've learned two things about you already. You don't follow instructions and you can't fight temptation." His smile grew from ear to

ear with what she assumed was some
sense of self-satisfaction

As he lifted his left hand to
welcome her inside, she noticed it was a
child-sized hand. It looked smooth and
soft. His right hand was a man's hand,
rough and calloused from hard work.

"I see you've discovered my gifted
hands." He held them both up.

"You sir, are a wonder." Sheridan
laughed the words more than stated
them, which seemed to encourage him.

He led Sheridan to a large bureau
made of cherry wood in a lobby at the
end of a long, wide corridor. She noticed
doors to rooms off both sides of the
passageway. One door was open
revealing an office. She imagined the
other doors were equally utilitarian,

except one labeled in great polished
brass letters: SHEPHERD'S CLOSET.

Once they entered the lobby, their
voices echoed and Sheridan looked up to
see all the way to the top of the three-
story building with grand staircases
curving up to each wing from the base.
She felt that she must try
to sketch it, however rough her
talent.

She stood at the bureau and pulled
out her credit card. The old man slapped
a ledger on its top. "I just need a room
for one day. I only plan to stay for a
good nap and let the fog lift. That is the
weirdest fog down the road."

"What fog? It looks clear enough to
me."

"That's what makes it so odd. It's
clear as a bell in this direction, but every

time I'd try to turn back toward the highway, I was in the deep fog again."

"Not to worry young lady."

He doesn't believe me.

He turned the book in her direction and glanced at the card. "Take things for granted too I see. You don't pay until you leave. The cost of your stay depends on what you do with your time here." Before she could grab it, he picked up her card, pulled out a large pair of scissors, and chopped it into four pieces.

"WHAT THE HECK DO YOU THINK YOU'RE DOING? YOU HAD NO RIGHT. I WANT A PHONE SO I CAN CALL MY FRIEND IN LINCOLN."

She took a deep breath. *Was the man deaf?* He continued what he was doing as if she'd said nothing.

"HEY" Sheridan grabbed his arm. "Phone"

"Heard ya, don't have one"

"So, if you don't want money, how do I get you to find me a phone and get me the heck out of here? Do I have to clean the Inn or help paint the church?" The sarcasm seemed lost on the host. *This cat and mouse game is over.*

"If I have to take a chance walking back to the interstate, I will. "

"Nope, Sheridan Easterly," was all he said. His eyes twinkled like a child playing gotcha. She could see the game was still on. "Oh, by the way, trying to walk back out of here would be a big risk. You'll just get turned around again and again and end up back here anyway."

"What is this place?"

"It's Hidden. Didn't you read the sign?"

Sheridan looked down at the ledger. It lay open to a clean page. It looked brand new, as did the pen that lay on top of it. The pen was a quill and the bottle of ink sat on the desktop next to the ledger along with a clean cloth for letting the excess ink drip before signing.

"It fits, it looks perfect for the Inn. I'll sign so I can get a nap, but I will be leaving as soon as that fog lifts." She signed her name in a Romanesque calligraphy, which was odd because she never studied the art.

He grabbed her large tote bag and waved his arm like a scoop signaling her to a grand staircase. "Practical woman, you travel light."

"Nothing much escapes you does it?" *Who is this idiot?*

"That's why they call me Catch."

Sheridan sighed. "I've traveled a lot -- Catch"

"That's what everybody calls me. I like it. Keeps me mysterious ya know?"

"Catch" She repeated. "And I suppose you think you've caught me in this tiny ghost town. I'll take a nap, but then I will go back down that road." There was more determination in her voice than in her mind.

"Did you know that your name, Sheridan, means to search? Are you a searcher, Sheridan?"

The old man had a bad habit of ignoring her no matter how angry she spat words at him.

He carried her tote up an ornate staircase. "Yes, I do know what my name means. How did you know my name? You called me by my name before I even signed your ledger."

"Tsk, tsk, little lady, You'll raise you blood pressure.

He pointed to an identity tag on her tote.

"Oh, that works too." A deep yawn escaped her as he opened the door to her room. "I guess I'm more tired than I thought. It's ridiculous to think you are keeping me prisoner. I will have to report that card stolen you know. You are in big trouble. That's frowned upon in Nebraska, you know."

"Okay." He said nothing else about it, just the one word, okay. *Does this man think he's untouchable?*

Sheridan noticed symbols on a wall plaque beside the door. "What is this all about?" Sheridan pointed to the plaque. "It looks like some kind of ancient, symbolic script."

She traced the symbols lightly with her fingers. The contrast of stiff, dry balsa wood against the smooth, polished wood of the door jam oddly seemed to fit. The symbols seemed familiar. "Hmm," She became the scientist again. "These symbols look like an ancient lost language. I've seen something like them somewhere."

"Well, it probably is authentic then."
Catch opened the door.

Sheridan peered into the room and gasped.

The contrast overwhelmed her. The new Early American style furnishings of the suite took her by surprise. The bathroom door stood open revealing all the gadgets of the most elegant hotels.

She made her way to the bathroom door and saw a walk-in, tiled shower, a large vanity complete with ornate mirror, built in hair dryer and plush rug.

The bathtub was large enough for two with body massaging jets. "Wow, this is something that I plan to take advantage of right away." She turned and smiled back at Catch. There were even bottles of her favorite brands of shampoo, lavender soaps, and candles setting on top of the marble counter.

Sheridan suddenly remembered the violation Catch perpetrated on her property.

The old man smiled, "Ye didn't think we were all backward did ye?" Catch seemed to have an endless repertoire of wisecracks to suit his chosen persona. He even added a hitch in his git-a-long to go with the old hillbilly.

Catch deposited the tote on a bench in a spacious closet.

"This doesn't make up for the card you destroyed."

"Expired"

"Expired? I have until the end of the month before it expires."

"Close enough."

"You're not talking so cocky now. Are you a little scared?"

"Ha, hardly"

Sheridan's energy drained so she had none left for arguing.

Looking around the room, Sheridan noticed a large portrait of the same odd flower as on the doorknocker. The room was like a dream from her youth. The color scheme and design of the room were in her favorite colors and styles.

Thinking of finally getting a chance to call Michael, she noticed there was no phone, television, or even a radio.

"Mr. Catch, I'd hoped for a telephone to call my friend in Lincoln. I don't see any in the room."

"No need to be so formal, just call me Catch." He drew in a breath. "We live simple here. We don't use phones, cars, or any of the things that make the world move so fast out there in the world."

"Don't you have a telephone downstairs for emergencies?"

"I'm afraid it isn't working, and I don't know when it'll be fixed. We have an old two-way radio. I'll see if we can get that to work." Catch replied. "You should get some rest and something to eat. You aren't expected today are you?"

"No, not particularly, my friend is used to me not checking in for a day or two. This isn't the first spot I've been in where I couldn't get a signal." *Why did I tell him that? Its not exactly information you give to someone you don't trust.*

Catch started to leave the room then looked back. "You are here because you are supposed to be here." He said almost in a whisper as he started out the door.

"What does that mean?"

He kept walking down the hall.

"WHAT DOES THAT MEAN?"

"Enjoy your room, you will find everything you need."

"Wait, don't I get a key?"

"No need for them around here." The old man turned his back to her and continued on his way.

Sheridan was alone in a lavish
room, done up as if they decorated it
exclusively for her. "How odd" She
made a deep sigh and looked around the
room.

A chair at the little table fit perfectly
under the doorknob. "There"

A bath sent warm relaxation through
her body. The water gently rolled over
each part as she twisted and nearly swam
in luxury.

Stepping out on the rug her feet
sank so deep her it tickled the top of her
feet. In the closet, a robe of pink silk slid
over her body like a caress.

Sheridan forgot her fears, her anger,
her frustration and fell into that welcome
calm she'd felt when she first arrived.

The flower portrait on the wall detailed more of the subject. The leaves were heart shaped with red veins. The petals were feathery and white. The artist had painted a yellow-gold stamen as if it shown like burnished gold.

She was curious about the designer who could have dreamed up such a beautiful theme for the Hide Inn.

Without thinking, Sheridan found herself sniffing at the painting as if she'd inhale the fragrance of the flower. Oddly enough, she found it smelled like a freshly cut lilac that the painter must have mixed into the paint.

She pulled her laptop from it's tote and filled two pages of her journal. Her report was a mess of the day's events. She started doubting her own impressions of the innkeeper. Maybe the card had expired. She typed it all into her notes and set it aside for her return to

Lincoln. She concluded with a note to Michael so she'd remember to tell him how she cared for him before hitting him with the craziness of that day.

Sheridan loved Michael and she knew he loved her. Their love was companionable rather than electric but just as heart felt and deep.

Her eyes drooped and soon she was nodding off in the desk chair. Her stomach groaned in protest, so she a banana from the immense fruit and cheese basket on the table by the sofa, then slid between the silk sheets of the huge soft bed. As she tried to think through the muddle of circumstances, she drifted in and out until the day gave way to slumber.

CHAPTER 2

Cook and Service.

Sheridan woke to a gentle breeze making a bit of hair tickle her forehead. The clean, spring air washing the room in freshness, then she sat bolt upright. "Who opened the window?"

Someone had opened the draperies and windows. *Catch! How did he get in?* The chair still blocked the door. Sheridan saw that Catch acted more like a buttinski butler than an innkeeper would.

She wasn't as concerned for her safety as for her privacy.

"I'm out of this town." She grabbed her stuff, her tote and left the room. The air whooshed with every angry step.

Catch sat in his easy chair in the lobby.

"Good morning, Sheridan. I imagine you are hungry, are you not?"

"Don't act so innocent. I'm not stupid. How did you get in my room? You can't just invade my room like that."

"I can get into any room in this building. A chair won't stop me."

"That doesn't give license to invade my privacy."

"You need your morning coffee" His grin made her want to slap him. "The Hidden Café is the next building down on this side of the street. We do have coffee here but I think Service and Cook would like the company. They can tell you some more about the town too."

"Was I talking in my sleep when you came in to open the windows?"

"Why would you ask that?"

"For one, I want you to apologize and promise you won't do it again." Spitting fire would have been too weak a description for her ire. "Never mind, I'm leaving now."

"Go ahead and try." He sighed as if indulging a child. "Yes, I did come in, open the drapes, and raise the window a bit. You seem the sort that likes the fresh air of the morning." Catch sounded impudent as if Sheridan were the offender.

"You have no intention of apologizing, do you?"

"If you want your morning coffee, the Hidden Café is next door." The old man seemed to scoot right past the subject.

Sheridan stalked out of the huge double doors directly toward the old, dirt road. The fog just past the sign swallowed her as soon as she stepped past the marker.

I'm going through and I'll find my way. I've survived sand storms in Egypt worse than this. Straight ahead, girl, one step in front of the other.

The first step engulfed her in the blinding whiteness of the thick cloud. She slid her right foot forward and then the left in front of it. Careful not to allow her body to turn in any direction that straight, she wished she could mark a straight line in front of her to follow. A half hour must have passed when the fog disappeared and she was looking at the Inn.

She tried time after time and ended up back on Street facing the inn. For once she had to admit Catch was right.

She slipped back just inside the fog and sat crying. Direction was useless, there wasn't any discernable. It was like the child in the forest who goes in circles repeatedly.

She went to the café to avoid Catch's smug smile.

Think of the devil may care old man now, if she had to stay in that inn, she would have to find his secret entry. Catch did pretty much whatever he wanted. A search of the room later might reveal his secret entry so she could block that as well.

Normally, Sheridan had cappuccino in the mornings, but the little café wasn't that up to the times. The menu on the wall offered coffee or a cup of tea. The old malt shop theme soothed her. She found a booth near a window facing the street and slid behind the table onto the cushioned bench.

The same flower decorated the eatery just as it did the inn. More interesting was the crystal version in a small crystalline bud vase on her table. It was exquisite. She picked it up and studied the intricacy of the object. She let her fingers slide lightly over each facet.

Holding it in front of the window, the sun glinted through the crystal bending the light into a kaleidoscope of colors. Impressive as the portrait in her room was, nobody could paint such beauty as the crystal.

"That's the actual size of the Lunis Flower. Isn't it beautiful?"

"There are real flowers like this?" Sheridan looked up at the waitress.

"Oh yes, it's a real flower. The Lunis flower is a living flower to which no artist has done justice. When you find it, your life will never be the same again."

"Where do I find one?"

"That is something you will discover on your journey."

"What journey?" She looked into the friendly face of the middle-aged woman whose gray hair held a few hints of its once dark brown hue. "I am here mostly by accident. I have some questions about the town, but then I must move on. I need to return to Lincoln as soon as that fog is gone."

"Fog; I haven't seen any fog. You aren't here by accident. I don't know how you got here, but it's not accidental."

"Why is everyone here so cryptic?"

"We don't mean to be. We answer your questions the only way we can."

"Then tell me why I am supposed to be here? Catch said the same thing."

"The only one to answer that is Shepherd. I know because everybody who comes here is here for a reason."

Sheridan felt it was the most direct answer she'd had so far, not satisfactory, but a full statement nonetheless.

"Back to the Lunis flower, it is very personal to all of us." The woman standing beside Sheridan's table said.

"You almost make it sound like it's a person."

Service giggled.

"I see, well I will ask more about that later." Sheridan knew pushing the subject probably wouldn't get her better answers. However, the woman seemed much friendlier and open that Catch. "I noticed your name tag says "Service." That surely isn't your name. Service is something you do."

Service smiled at Sheridan as she slid into the facing bench. "I love being called Service. It's not just something I do Sheridan, it defines what I love to be and do. My other name is Vida. But please, do call me Service."

"Okay, as long as you don't call me Search."

"Agreed," Service chuckled.

Sheridan took mental notes about the people she met and the surroundings. She would journal them later. Hidden held deeper secrets than anywhere she'd been, including Egypt. As long as the fog kept her trapped, she'd just as well find investigate. "It's kind of quiet around here isn't it?"

"Yes, we all love the silence, except for the Angel Choir, whom we all love to hear. Their sound is so perfect." Service hands touched her chin as she closed her eyes.

"I've heard them. When I first arrived, they were like a soothing whisper. I can't wait to hear them up close."

"That won't happen on this side of the street. Um, they chant in prayer, not as performance." Service looked as if she was covering her first statement. "What can I get you Sheridan?"

"You know my name?"

"We all do. It's a short five blocks in this town. You know small towns; we almost know what someone is thinking before they do. It doesn't take long to pass news."

"That's true enough." Sheridan laughed. "I'll just have a cup of tea."

"Good choice, do you want any eggs?"

"No, just the tea"

"Coming up, do you care if I join you? It's pretty quiet in here and I'd love to chat."

"No, not at all, I have a lot of questions about Hidden."

"Well, that's a subject I love to talk about."

A man called out from the kitchen. "Hello Sheridan, can I make you?" She figured he was the man they called Cook

"I'm just having tea, thank you." She responded smiling at a well-groomed, middle-aged man with a boat shaped white hat on his head.

"Ah, come on now," he pleaded. "Give an old guy an order for some eggs and toast. You look like you could eat them. You're such a small thing, it'll make you grow."

"Yes, out," Sheridan held her hands out in front of her stomach and puffed her cheeks. "Okay, I give up. Give me eggs, toast, and tea please."

"That's a girl. I've already fired up the griddle. Three orders coming up"

"Are you joining us too, Cook?" Sheridan asked.

"Why not." he motioned to the rest of the empty tables and the equally empty street outside. Then wiped his hands on a towel he took out of his apron and went into the kitchen to finish cooking their breakfast.

Service brought the tea and sat across the table from Sheridan.

"So Sheridan the searcher, what is it you search for? Do you search for love, or perhaps restoration?"

"What an odd thing to ask, Service."

Cook joined them with their breakfast. "Service is a romantic. I think she always has been a Juliet looking for her Romeo." He nudged Service with his meaty arm and smiled down at the woman in a way that told Sheridan Service wasn't the only romantic in the café.

"Uh, huh," was Sheridan's only reply, but it hit its target. "So, I take it neither of you were from here to start with."

"None but maybe Catch and Shepherd. I think they have always been."

Sheridan caught the way Cook dropped his sentence.

"Well, Sheridan," Service insisted. "Give us a story."

"Well, if a story is what you two like, I'll tell you a true one."

"Oh, do tell," both chimed together.

"First," Sheridan enquired. "You tell me about this thing between the two of you. Uh, huh; I've noticed your looks and jabs."

"Oh, we are very fond of each other. We are very in like and that's as far as it goes. Nothing beyond what you see here. Now no more stalling, tell us about your life before Hidden." Service seemed to be the pushier one of the two.

"I am an anthropologist. The last few years I've been teaching at the University of Nebraska in Lincoln. However, the past six weeks I've been on a book signing tour and getting information for a new book. I ended up in Hidden because of that bad fog and thought I'd find out a little about the town. So, that's why I'm being snoopy." Sheridan ended her brief summary.

"Good try Sheridan, but that's not who you are. That's a job description." Cook remarked. "We want to know about you, not your job."

The jolly man looked straight into Sheridan's eyes. She felt as if he was searching inside her brain with his stare. His hazel eyes looked for the essence of Sheridan as if it were a treasure.

Sheridan took a deep cleansing breath and blew it out. "Okay," She looked down at the tea in her cup that shimmered with a surprising reflection of part of her face. "I was married before I went to Egypt. I met Mark at a lecture he was giving in Lincoln about his archeological missions in Egypt. He'd been following the trail the Holy family took on their way to Egypt after King Herod's decree to kill all the young Hebrew boys. I fell in love with Mark while I was sitting there in my chair."

Sheridan was back in that time and place as Service and Cook seemed to fade. "He was so driven to find physical proof that Jesus traveled through that path in Egypt. That's what he did. It was as if his life wasn't going to be complete until he found that proof. It was his passion and sincerity that touched me that day." Sheridan chuckled. "His good looks didn't hurt either. He was handsome."

Sheridan sighed deeply. "God blessed that man with a physique and face that made a girls heart drum in her ears. It did mine. What I didn't know was that he was casting glances at me.

He said later he looked at me and thought I was someone he wanted to get to know fast. He claimed he was in a hurry to court me and get me back to Egypt as his wife." She took a deep breath.

"Go on, what about Egypt." Service's remark made Sheridan jump.

"Whew, I kind of got lost in my story."

"We noticed." Her companions chimed in unison.

Sheridan looked at them and they were smiling like a couple of children.

"Oh Okay," she teased. "We fell in love. Less than a year later, we were married and back in Egypt where he'd been digging. I worked with the people of the Bedouin tribe we lived with.

They are so open to everyone. They don't even worry about who you are. The Bedouin people accept everyone with unbelievable hospitality."

Sheridan smiled back at Cook and Service lowering her voice as if she was telling them a secret. "There was an elderly woman there who took us in as if we were her own children. She was the oldest woman of the camp and all other women went to her for advice on everything from bread recipes to how to pleasure their husbands in bed." Sheridan snickered.

"She was so sweet. Her name was Sarai. Oops, is Sarai. She's still there and very much alive. Anyway, we became best friends. She practically moved into our tent when we found out I was expecting a baby."

Sheridan's face dropped as she remembered the pain later when she found out she'd lost the baby.

"The tribe was Jewish." She looked up at her audience. "You remember the lost tribes of Israel? They aren't lost, not to the Jews anyway. But the Levites mingled with the other tribes. The family of Levites that composed the nomadic tribes we followed stretched from modern Israel throughout Egypt.

God gave them the duty of watching after artifacts that He was afraid would become idols. God entrusted them with artifacts such as the Staff of Moses."

Sheridan snickered to herself. "Many people, including ministers, don't think about the fact that the book of James, in the Bible, is a letter to all the tribes of Israel. The author wrote those letters long after the tribes were supposedly lost. Isn't it funny that we consider them lost just because we can't track them? Ah, well anyway, that's what Mark was looking for. He didn't want to expose the artifacts they protected. He just wanted proof the Holy family had been there."

"It turns out that when they left Israel; they were assisted by these Levite nomads who guided them from one family group to the next. Mark had already followed that route and was in Egypt on the final leg of his search." She took a deep breath. "I didn't tell you he was an archeologist did I?"

"Sure you did, or at least alluded to it. You loved him very much didn't you?" Service asked softly.

"Yes, I think he will always be the love of my life. That's why Michael has never asked me to marry him, I think."

"Michael, who is he?"

"Michael is a Dean of Historical Studies at the university. He's never been married. I think he's too married to his work. But, we've been dating for about a year now. He was the one who pushed me to write my book Living Bedouin after my doctoral thesis. That was such a journey back to that time with Mark. It was so cathartic that I finally had to face the horrible things that were chasing me all those years."

"What horrible things were those?" Cook asked as Service nudged him.

Sheridan hung her head. "That's where Mark was killed."

"We had gone to the dig. He had found some Aramaic script on one of the walls in a small chamber. It wasn't deep, but it was hard to get to the chamber. I had to crawl through a very narrow passage on my belly to get to it. Mark had mixed feelings about taking me in there. I was just getting through my first trimester and he wanted me to see it. Nevertheless, he was afraid for the baby and me. I was the one who insisted it would be fine." Sheridan eyes started to tear up. "It was like stepping back in time. We couldn't read it, but we had experts who read dead languages back in the states." Tears filled Sheridan's eyes and she used a napkin to wipe her face.

"Mark knew enough about ancient Aramaic to know that's what it was. He took all kinds of pictures. He sent me back out of the chamber with a memory card full of pictures of the writing and the inside of the chamber. I didn't get more than a few steps. I don't remember it to this day, but they said an insurgent pushed me off my feet with his horse and threw a pipe bomb in the cave where Mark was. Well it wasn't really a cave."

Sheridan's voice quavered and her hands started shaking. Her speech slurred and she couldn't find her words.

She was looking down at drops making ripples in her teacup. "That's when I lost them both. Mark and the baby died that day and I woke up in Cairo hospital weeks later"

"Sheridan," Service was hugging her. "Come back to us sweetie. You are safe. Nobody can hurt or take anything away from you here. Do you hear me Sheridan?"

The fugue passed and Service voice filtered through. Sheridan hated when she lost herself. She felt embarrassed.

"I'm so sorry. I still seem to suffer from some posttraumatic episodes."

She pushed her cup away as though it was her past. "That's enough about me anyway. You, tell me about Hidden please. I haven't seen any other streets except, well, Street. Are any of these buildings homes? Where are the children?" Her mind was racing, and she needed something to help her back.

"Are you sure Sheridan? Why don't you just drink your tea and relax for a while?"

"No, please. If you talk about something else, it helps me come out of this stupid haze. It's like talking to my thoughts and changing direction."

Service nodded. "Okay, I get that. All of the buildings are shops, but most do have an apartment on the second floor so we live comfortably. We don't like many possessions. They just cause too much worry. In fact, we depend so well on each other that we don't even need to use money."

"How unusual and refreshing," Sheridan's mind went back to Egypt again for a moment. "The only other people I've known that live such a simple life are the Bedouins." She shook her head to come back to the present again. "How do you get supplies? I haven't seen or even smelled any farms or crops. Are there any children living here?"

Cook inserted himself into the conversation. "Some supplies are delivered, but most we take care of ourselves. Most of us don't have any children and those who do; their children are all gone now."

"Ah," Sheridan's mind cleared and she was back in the present. "So is this like a retirement community, or commune?"

"That's something we'll explain later." Service cut the conversation short. "It's time for a quick sandwich for lunch, and then you are off to visit the rest of the town."

"Oh, Service, I am much too full from breakfast. I didn't realize we'd chatted so long."

"Well, let me give you a sandwich to take along." Cook said. "I have your ham with bacon and cheddar all ready. I even put some sweet mustard on it for you."

"How did you know that is my favorite sandwich?"

"Is it? Well, it is good for you that I made you my specialty." Cook replied with a smile.

"There is something under the layers of Hidden I am determined to discover." Sheridan taunted them both. She'd hoped to get some kind of response either affirming or denying her remark. She'd wanted them to reveal something.

"On your way now girl," Service smiled and gave her a little nudge on the back. "Oh, and Sheridan, please stay on this side of the street. The Angel Choir likes their solace and we have a sort of invisible barrier that we all try to respect. Only Tailor crosses over to take them new robes."

"Okay, I'll try." Sheridan replied with a puzzled look back at the two. "I'll be back later. But, if the Angel Choir is not outside, why can't I cross Street and check out the buildings?

"Not outside? Sheridan, look and listen the choir does that all day long. They will not notice you or break their bond to speak to you." Service tried to explain.

"That sounds kind of rude." Sheridan retorted.

"It won't once you have a better understanding of Hidden." Cook finished the conversation and opened the door for Sheridan. It seemed Cook had the final word on the matter.

Sheridan left the café realizing they had revealed a lot to her in the last moments of the conversation. However, what they revealed only created more questions. She was beginning to see a pattern developing. Each citizen she spoke to seemed to develop a very quick, friendly, or at least somewhat personal relationship with her. Yet, none of them gave her answers that didn't bring forth bigger questions. She felt as if they were examining her.

Sheridan took another step past the stoop of the café more determined than ever to find Hidden's essence.

Chapter 3: Angel Choir and Tailor

Once outside the café, Sheridan had some time to think about what Cook and Service said, or rather didn't say. *Talk about jumbled information.*

The Lunis flower intrigued her more than any other possible artifact she might find in Hidden.

It was then she noticed the beautiful harmony of voices coming from across the street. She watched a group of singers stroll up the sidewalk toward the Angel Choir Chapel.

Each wore an ivory colored, silk robe. Their faces covered with hoods or some with more of a scarf. Sheridan had a sense of being miles away from the group.

Tempted as she was to cross over and try to strike up a conversation, she remembered the Cook and Service warning. As an anthropologist, she knew the importance of respecting a culture's boundaries.

She watched, as they got closer to the chapel. They never once looked her direction. They didn't seem to notice anything outside their group.

Sheridan studied their uniformity of dress and realized they weren't all the same. Each robe bore its own design of jewels and style. Some wore smocks over skirts, some were full robes, while yet others were tunics and pants. Each had a hood or scarf, and all were made of ivory silk.

She saw jeweled designs on each one. Some costumes encrusted with jewels and tatted lace, while other members clothing were much less lavish.

The only visible parts she could see were their hands that they clasped in front of their faces as if in prayer. She stood in awe at the various skin tones. Every possible color of skin in the world walked in that group. It was a moment of divine realization for Sheridan. Tears welled up in her eyes.

She watched to see where they entered the chapel. She'd expected them to go through a door to the back of the building. Instead, their numbers deleted slowly and inexplicably.

She tried to cross the street against advice and found herself back where she started. "I'm hallucinating." She said aloud. "What did they give me in that café?"

Suddenly she felt she was not in an earthly place anymore. Was Hidden a commune serving up hallucinogenic mushrooms in their tea? She looked across the street at the Angel Choir Chapel and then behind her at the café.

For a moment, she was soaring on a plane above her own consciousness. She reached for the handle to the café door and had to grab for the outside jamb instead. She'd never felt more outside of herself. She felt as if she would collapse. Then she felt the wood under her feet and returned to her body.

She felt hands steady her as she teetered. "Sheridan, you look pale as a ghost. I think you'd better come back in and sit for a little while." She heard Vida's voice.

The inside of the café was warm and friendly feeling, but Sheridan didn't know what or who to trust. "What did you give me? I've never felt like that before in my life." Sheridan's voice shook.

"Just some tea and breakfast," Cook replied sounding concerned.

"Yes, honey, what happened to you out there?"

"Service, let's get her to sit down before we grill her." They led her to a chair near the door.

"I could have sworn I was hallucinating. The Angel Choir disappeared into the chapel through the wall or something. I tried to cross the street and I ended up here. Then I got woozy. I've never felt that way before. Not even when I was in the hospital with a concussion and my equilibrium was off because of an inner ear injury."

"When was that, dear? Maybe you're having some trouble with your equilibrium again."

Service asked but didn't wait for an answer. "I wouldn't worry about the Angel Choir. I think they have a secret entrance in an alcove over there. I saw you try to cross the street and then you started stumbling and looked like you lost direction. The next thing we knew, you were back here."

Sheridan saw that Service was an excitable woman.

"Here is some water." Cook sat the glass of clear liquid on the table in front of her.

Sheridan hesitated and then thought about the real possibility that what Service said was true. It certainly made more sense than what she'd been thinking. She took a sip and felt the refreshing cold liquid. She drank the rest of the water down as if she'd been back in the desert.

"Feeling better?" Service and Cook both spoke up in unison.

For the first time, she took her mind off the things around her and thought of the people. Hidden was a curious place but the people were even more of a mystery. They were her target to study, but she felt drawn into their lives much in the same way Sarai's clan welcomed her in the desert.

Sarai had been her most trusted friend in Egypt. The elder woman took the roles of mother, sister, confidant, and counselor for her there. Sheridan loved her dearly. Sarai not only welcomed Sheridan as one of her own, she had adopted Mark as well. In fact, Sarai saw to it that every member of the tribe, from elder to infant, welcomed them as family.

However, it wasn't the same. In many ways, it seemed the same, but that scared her. It was as if the people of Hidden were somehow surreal, just as Hidden was a mystery of place and time. Sheridan wondered if there was any way to separate Hidden and its residents in her mind. The town made the people as much as the people made the town. She thanked Cook and Service and stepped back out into the fresh air.

She continued down the wooden walk stopping by some businesses, none of which accepted money for their wares. Finally, she was near the end of the five-block town. The last limestone building was a Tailor's shop. The display window well decorated with swatches of ivory silk, various laces, and jewels.

Sheridan felt herself clashing in her red shirt and blue jeans standing in front of that store. There were no racks of clothing. Instead, it was full of the ivory silk cloth and a few sewing machines.

Sheridan entered the shop almost as if it were a church considering the spiritual sense of the choir. She opened the door tenuously. The opulence that surrounded her was breath taking.

The shop seemed a complete departure from the simplicity the town's people guarded so closely. However, judging from the appearance of the Angel Choir, the richness of their dress fit easily into their surroundings.

Not seeing anyone, Sheridan called out "Hello?"

A head popped out from behind a shelf. The man looked a little shocked. "I'm sorry Mrs. Easterly. I didn't expect you'd be stopping by my shop."

The middle-aged man was short but stout. His arms were muscular from hours of lifting bolts of fabric, cutting, and sewing. He had very little fat on him, which surprised Sheridan. Most people she knew who sat for most of their work tended to thicken in the middle. Obviously that was an assumption she needed to reassess.

"I'm sorry I didn't mean to spook you. I simply couldn't help but come in here and look over your merchandise. I saw the Angel Choir strolling across the street. Did you design all of the clothes? They're gorgeous."

"Yes, each choir member's garment is designed especially for them."

"I'm sorry," Sheridan held out her hand, "you all know my name but I would like to know yours too, please."

"Tailor"

Sheridan smiled and suppressed an urge to giggle. Fitting, I should have guessed that. She'd noticed the boxes on the shelves filled with gems from amethyst to diamond. Even the threads were silver and gold.

"Are those real? I mean diamonds, emeralds, onyx beads, and gold and silver thread?"

"Yes, they are very real."

Sheridan looked at his hands. She could see the little scars from years of needle punctures. There was a row of thimbles lined carefully on the top of the counter, but she doubted that he used them often. She remembered her mother thought they got in her way. A smile crossed Sheridan's face.

"Oh," the short, stout man said nervously, "pardon me." Tailor said as he put his hands in his ample pockets.

"No, don't hide them. I was thinking of how my mother hated thimbles. She would understand every facet of your work. All of it seemed to be lost on me."

For the first time since she had entered his shop, she saw Tailor noticeably relax. His shoulders released from their locked position near his ears, his hands opened, and his facial muscles smoothed out.

"I'm an anthropologist, Tailor, and I like to collect remnants or artifacts from the places I visit. Is there a chance that you could make me a simple robe?" She saw the doubt in his expression. "I journeyed from Israel to Egypt on an expedition and I brought back a sample of each style of dress worn by the tribes. I find they help me in my lectures and have so much to say about the people's culture in each place. The last small town I stopped at, here in Nebraska, had a quilting group with their own unique quilting pattern. They even had it patented because they designed it as a group. I have one of those quilts to take back with me to the university."

"I'm sorry, Sheridan," the middle aged man said, "but these materials are exclusively for the choir. They are not to leave Hidden. The very nature of these garments would cause the greedy ones to try to enter here. They cannot come to Hidden. It is not allowed."

"Tailor," Sheridan tried to reassure him. "I do understand. These are priceless and rare. The thread count of the silk alone must be worth a lot on the market outside Hidden." Sheridan continued. "I respect your boundaries. The knowledge of those priceless gems anywhere else would invite greed. I will not even mention the riches of your shop or of this town. I understand how dangerous that could be. I am curious about one thing you said, though Tailor,"

Sheridan continued. "You specified the 'greedy ones' as if they were a unique group. You also said they would try to enter Hidden, but cannot. I didn't notice any gates, no trespassing signs, or any security at all when I came here. How do you keep the 'greedy ones' out"?

"You were of no threat. You belong here, Sheridan. We don't need security at the gates, so to speak, to protect us. We have something much more powerful."

"What is that?"

Tailor became visibly nervous again. "I've revealed too much. You will know when it is time. I can't say anymore."

Sheridan had learned not to push people. If she did she'd lose their trust and with it their willingness to reveal the uniqueness of their society. The cryptic remark made her nervous. His guarded responses were ominous.

The secrets of Hidden were disconcerting. Sheridan felt it was all very involved with her, but nobody wanted to explain.

"Thank you Tailor, you have been very gracious and enlightening." Sheridan smiled at him and he seemed to relax again. "I am curious about your name. I know this is a tailor's shop. Is that why you call yourself Tailor?"

"Taylor with a 'y' is my given name, but here I spell it T-a-i-l-o-r. I like the way we all use names that reflect our passions."

"Well, that makes Catch an odd duck indeed." Sheridan chuckled.

An odd shadow of displeasure came over Tailor's face. "Catch is more than an odd duck Sheridan. Don't be too taken with him. Catch is a trickster. He can mess with your mind in many ways and do things that none of us can begin to imagine until we see it. He can be...I'll just say menacing."

"Well, I've certainly experienced his difficult side. To tell you the truth, I find Catch kind of fun. He's quite a character." Sheridan chuckled "I'll be going now. I've been down this side of Street and visited so many of your shopkeepers. I think I'll head back to the Inn." Sheridan said. "I'll try not to let Catch get to me."

"Oh Sheridan, don't mistake that witty humor as charm. He can be charming and all the while he will seduce you into a world of deceit."

"I will be cautious. Thank you, Tailor."

Tailor waved from the door of his shop as she left. She could swear she saw a grin on his face. She felt satisfied he'd actually enjoyed her company in spite of her initial sense of intrusion.

Sheridan walked back up the street to the Inn with a determination in her step. *I'm getting to the bottom of this nonsense. And, I'm going to get in touch with Michael.*

Chapter 4: Things

Sheridan walked into the lobby of
the Inn looking for her host. She found
Catch in a room full of odd collections
of objects placed carefully around the
huge banquet room.

"Oh, hello Catch. I was looking for
you."

"I kind of gathered that from the
racket you were making when you came
into the room."

Sheridan looked down at the thick
carpet under her feet. She knew she
hadn't said anything or called for him.
He must have a high sense of people
arriving at his Inn. She suspected most
Innkeepers had such an antenna. Could it
really be much different than noticing a

slight difference in your own home when someone opens a door? Sheridan asked herself.

"I'm sorry, I didn't realize I was making noise, but wow, what is this room all about?" She waved her hand around the room at the odd collections.

"Well, I see you are intent on interrupting my reading." Catch growled.

She hadn't noticed he was reading until he mentioned it. "I'm sorry Catch."

He laid a book down on the sofa where he'd been sitting. Sheridan looked at the book cover but there was no title on it, not even an author's name. It did have some odd symbols on each corner. One corner had a scorpion, the second a coiled snake, another had a locust with wings open and the final corner looked like the head of a vulture. In the center of the book's cover was a skull inside a starburst.

"Wow that must be a disturbing book."

"Not really." Catch sighed in resignation to her interruptions. 'It is a hobby. I've also studied some of the deadliest cults and cultures. Amazingly, some of the deadliest societies haven't been tribes of head hunters."

Catch's tone changed quickly from a disturbing; almost whisper to an easily audible instructor. "As to your question, this room is like a museum of previous guests. They all come in with things they think they can't do without and they all leave them behind when they go, just as you will."

"Catch; you and Tailor are beginning to scare me. What have I walked into here?"

"It's just a place, Sheridan, nothing here for you to concern yourself about."

Sheridan shrugged and walked around the room looking at tables full of electronics that could tell a story of the history and progression of technology. From the end of a table set a small abacus and, other tables full of watches, laptops, PDA's, and all sorts of paraphernalia.

A cabinet held items that had probably been very dear to the previous owners. She saw small teacups and saucers hand painted with family crests, antique bronzes, gold encrusted statuettes, and busts likely of some family's member. Some of the items that set around the floor of the room were so large that Sheridan questioned how people managed to carry them into the town.

Items, like a marble statue of Grecian design and an old Hollywood camera standing like a monolith of the silent movie era, may possibly travel. However, it wasn't likely that anyone coming to Hidden would have brought them.

According to Catch one visitor or another left behind even the tables, bureaus and display cabinets.

"Very funny Catch, truthfully, where did you get all this stuff? There are some valuable and ancient items here. Nobody is going to carry a giant Chinese urn around. Does one of those books of yours teach you how to steal riches of the world?" Sheridan laughed.

"Sheridan, I can't answer your questions. I didn't lie to you. I can't explain people's behavior. Some people carry so much on their backs just trying to protect things like this. Then when they leave, they leave it all behind."

"So you are into some kind of acquisitions?"

"In a fashion, I suppose you could say that. There is a lot of stuff here. I wish I could get rid of it, but it seems to have its purpose because Shepherd won't allow me to dispose of any of it. He says it serves to tell a story to those who enter here about the lack of importance of the items they carry. None of those who visit this room gets the idea until they go on their way to the next stop."

"Next stop, what do you mean, next stop?"

"Sheridan, I am an old man. I say things wrong sometimes. I guess I should have said when you leave here."

Catch was old but Sheridan had the feeling he definitely said what he meant. "Ah," was all she said, nodding her head. She'd heard Shepherd mentioned before, and remembered the Shepherd's Closet in the front hall.

"Who is Shepherd? His name's come up a couple times now. He must have a lot of authority around here."

"You'll find out in due time," Catch hissed.

Sheridan got the impression Catch resented Shepherd somehow. "Well, that is not why I was looking for you anyway. Is there a map of the area that will help me find that Lunis Flower?"

"There is a map of the area, but it doesn't point out the location of the Lunis Flower. I hate that damn weed." Catch snapped loudly.

"Whoa, I've been hearing about this flower since I got here and now you act like it's poison." Sheridan backed off as if to escape his wrath.

"Everyone is such a damn broken record," he grumbled. 'It's as if all there is in Hidden is that stupid flower and Shepherd. What about this inn, it's not shabby you know. What about my pride and joy?"

"Wow, Catch. I'm talking about a plant that I haven't even seen except in pictures and the crystal sculptures over at the café. It seems to be an important part of your town's story. Shepherd is another part of that story and so are you and the Inn. I don't know why you are biting my head off.

Your Inn seems like it's a shrine to the flower. I mean look around you." Sheridan slowly stepped back into Catch's space with her own indignation.

She could see Catch exert almost measurable effort to calm himself. The red-hot anger faded slowly into his usual rough, fleshy color. "I'm sorry Sheridan. I'm out of sorts today. Of course, it's silly for me to be so upset over that flower."

Catch rummaged through some items in the drawer of an ancient dresser near the couch where he'd been sitting. He handed her a map on a parchment scroll. "That's about all I have for a map."

Sheridan unrolled it. The map was an ancient cartographer's sketch of the area. It didn't seem to give a lot for distances, but the maker had drawn a meadow with trees and a lake, mountains with a valley below, and other points of interest with names for each written beside the sketch.

"This is it?" Sheridan asked.

"Yup"

"Catch, answer my question please. What is this place? I've asked one question after another and none seems to get proper answers. If I do get answers, they bring about more unanswered questions." She retorted holding up the map. "This for instance," she pointed to the map "is ancient and can't have much bearing on the lay of the land now."

"Sheridan," Catch raised his voice like a teacher suffering a belligerent student. "What would you consider a proper answer? It's a place, a stop in your journey and we may be different to what you're used to, but honey, we are all treating you well aren't we?"

"Well, yes, you are all treating me very well. I can't understand that. I come into your village completely unexpected. Nobody seems surprised by my appearance even though I haven't seen another newbie anywhere. What's more, I have not been able to make any contact with Michael, or anything of the outside world. You must admit, Catch, I have a few reasons to be curious."

"Sheridan, you look at this room with all of its oddities and articles, and you know there have been many other visitors. It's not hard to hear someone coming up our road. Once we know someone is coming, we make it our business to get to know them very quickly. We tend to communicate in our short five blocks." The old man took control of the conversation again.

"I think you're just getting tired from the day." His voice softened and took a more concerned tone. "Why don't you go to your rooms and freshen up? Your dinner will be in your suite when you're done."

"Suite," Sheridan echoed. "Catch, I have a room. As nice as it is, I don't think it qualifies as a suite."

"No dear, you do have a suite."

"How many rooms and where do I find a door? I didn't see one." She wasn't being belligerent or even irritable anymore. She realized just how tired she was after her long day. She was especially weary from her battle of wits with Catch.

"The door is behind a curtain, you just didn't see it is all. You were so exhausted when you arrived, and I must say, a bit preoccupied with your situation."

"Situation?"

"You were disturbed about not being able to contact your man friend. We are pretty much self contained and don't use modern communication."

"I guess I am a little caught up in the mysteries of Hidden." She took a deep breath and let it out in a rush. "I'll look for that door. I am grateful for yourhospitality Catch, but I do feel stuck here and things seem kind of weird, like with this room." She pointed to the room full of articles left behind by others.

"It's not a problem. I've heard it all before." Catch soothed.

Sheridan sighed weakly wondering how Catch had taken her indignation and turned it into a feeling of guilt for being ungrateful. He was a cagy one. She remembered what Tailor had told her about Catch. However, she thought, Tailor was just as elusive about answering her questions. "Ah, heck with it; tomorrow is another day for solving dilemmas." Sheridan made her way to her room and threw back the curtain.

Chapter 5: The Suite

The door opened easily to the hidden rooms. Sheridan entered cautiously as if she were expecting an ogre of some kind on the other end.

The first room astounded her. In fact, it was impossible.

Sheridan looked into the living room of her home in Lincoln. Even the gray, floral, traditional style sofa and matching chairs, the antique brass lamps with umbrella shades, knick-knacks such as her mother's prized cup and saucer collection. Every little detail was identical to her home. She stepped in closing the door behind her.

She looked down at the pale gray rug under her feet. The smell of the room still held the smell of her mother's cooking. It smelled like Sheridan's favorite meal, reserved for special occasions.

Walking from one room to the next, there was not one difference from her house. She looked out the window to see Hidden's Street with the Angel Choir Chapel on the other side.

There was the hallway leading to a downstairs bedroom decorated as if her mother was still alive. Sheridan had never redecorated the room after her mother's death, except to send her mother's clothes to a shelter. She'd sent them all except one piece. She ran to the closet and threw open the door.

All the clothing was gone but for the one remaining robe. Sheridan's head reeled as she sat for a moment on the blue striped bedside chair.

"How?" her whisper was like a loud gong to her own ears.

Standing, Sheridan moved mechanically up the stairs that led to a second floor. She looked into the three bedrooms, one of which was an exact replica of her own back in Lincoln. She noticed the telephone beside her bed on the simple mission style table.

Sheridan sat on the bed and grabbed the receiver. There was a dial tone. She dialed her home number just to see if it would ring or if she would get one of those messages saying she was calling from within her own house. To her surprise, she heard Michael's voice on the other end.

"Michael, I can't believe it. I didn't think I could get in touch with you. Everything is so mixed up."

"I'll say," he replied. He sounded relieved. "We're here for you honey, we want you to come back to us."

"Oh Michael, I want nothing more than to do just that. I'm stuck in a place called Hidden. They said I couldn't talk to you. You won't believe it but I'm in my own bedroom at home speaking to you on my own phone. I know it's not my real home, but it's as if they moved it here." Sheridan realized she was rambling.

"Honey, it's okay." She heard her sister's voice soothing her over the line. We'll wait for you. We know it's hard for you, but we are so relieved to hear your voice. We pray for you every day. Pastor is here too."

"I'm confused." Sheridan was crying. The line filled with static and then went dead. They must have heard about the thick fog. She'd only been out of touch for a comparatively short time. Some of her trips were much longer.

"Catch!" she screeched. "I want to know what the hell is going on. You said there were no phones in Hidden. I just spoke to my family. They are in my house in Lincoln. I am standing in my own house here. What is going on and why did you lie? What kind of set up is this?"

Anger ruled as she walked into her kitchen. Adrenaline coursed through her. Catch stood near the table uncovering dishes. He even had on her mother's apron. On the table was a meal of stuffed Cornish hen, asparagus spears, and new potatoes with peas in butter. A green salad and desert of chocolate moose in small dishes sat above the plate like eyes. It was the final insult to her psyche. Crossing the line into serving her mother's and her favorite special meal was more than she could handle. She swept it all off on the floor in a fit of rage, slapped Catch, and tugged the apron until he had to undo the ties in the back or get a nasty bruise.

The young woman planted her feet wide apart with her hands on her hips.

"Catch, I want an answer to this right now." She shook with rage, trying to slow her breathing seemed impossible. Sheridan was in a battle for sanity.

"I'm glad you were able to speak to your family. I hope you feel better now." Sheridan knew her anger wasn't lost on him; he simply refused to acknowledge it. "You want to clean up your mess?"

"What!" Sheridan screamed. "This is too weird." She ran from the kitchen to the living room and flung open the front door. It opened to the outside of the Inn. If she stepped forward, she would be on the wooden sidewalk of Street.

Sheridan fainted.

When she woke up in her room at the inn, Service was sitting on the edge of her bed wiping her brow with a soft, damp cloth.

"Service, I'm so glad to see you. I had the oddest dream. It was insane, but so real."

"Sheridan, it wasn't a dream. You really were there. You fainted and Catch called for me because he felt I would be the friendliest face when you woke up."

"It wasn't a dream? I don't understand. I was in my own house, but I wasn't. It was exactly like my home in

Lincoln. How did I get back into this room? Service, what is this place?"

"First of all, Catch carried you back into this room. The rest of your questions are more difficult to answer." Service grasped Sheridan's hand lightly. "Call me Vida when I'm not in the café. I feel more like Vida when I'm not there."

"Vida," Sheridan drew in a deep breath and exhaled slowly. "Please don't confuse me anymore. I need real answers. There is no way I was just in my home in Lincoln. So what was it, or is it?"

"Okay, well I can't guarantee an easy answer or even satisfactory, but here goes. The Inn is a kind of passage. Hidden is a stop of sorts. Kind of like a bus stop. When Shepherd comes, he will be able to lay aside all of your doubts. That's really all I can tell you. You must learn to trust without question with some, and to question other's motives at every turn. You've had some warnings already. Please listen to them. Catch can seem like a friendly old guy, but you really need to be careful of his deceptions."

"Vida, was I in a duplicate of my own home? Yes or no?" Sheridan was tired of people side stepping her questions with one kind of philosophical non-answer, or social platform that answered exactly nothing.

"Yes," Vida answered bluntly. However, she wouldn't or couldn't expand her answer to how. "It is not beyond Catch's capabilities. Now I really can not say anymore."

Sheridan didn't press the subject. Vida looked around nervously as if she was afraid someone might overhear her.

Then she whispered close to Sheridan's ear. "Shepherd is also able to do magical kinds of things that I don't understand. I just have to know I trust Shepherd. Is that a better answer for you?" Vida had tears from frustration and, Sheridan suspected, the sting of Sheridan's own ire.

"Trust," Sheridan contemplated the word. "Who should I trust? I found Catch reading a book with weird symbols on the cover. The symbols looked...evil. I know some people get off on that stuff, but he was studying it like a textbook." Sheridan took a deep breath and grabbed Vida by the shoulders. "Vida, he said that he likes to study deadly cults. It bothered me but some people are into the study of stuff like demonology or witchcraft without being a part of them."

Sheridan shook her head as tears rolled down her face. "But, how do I know you aren't a part of his deceptions. There is something unnatural about this place. You could be warning me about Catch just to lure me in too. I don't know whom to trust. I don't know if I can even trust myself."

"Oh," Vida paused to hand tissues to Sheridan and both wiped the tears from their eyes. "Oh dear child, I know you have been through a lot. It's not surprising to me at all that you are confused. Why don't you get some sleep?"

They each blew their noses. The sound started them laughing. It released much of the stress between them and they were friends again.

"Is there another place I can stay Vida, I feel so confused." Sheridan paused trying to decide how to verbalize her thoughts honestly without being insulting. I'm still not sure whom to trust here. The whole town is like something out of an odd science fiction movie. Some of you say not to trust Catch, and sometimes I wonder if I can trust those telling me not to trust another. Do you understand what I mean?"

Vida didn't seem upset. She smiled as if she understood Sheridan's confusion. "Sheridan, we've all been a little bit, oh what should I say? We haven't revealed a lot about ourselves or about Hidden. I wish I could wave a wand and help you see, but I can't. The thing is you are a woman of faith, and you are a questioner as well. Those are good things Sheridan. Hidden is a place in between life and a dream so to speak. You are not in danger staying at the Inn."

Sheridan looked deep into Vida's eyes for the woman she knew as Service. Service was there just as Vida. She was one in the same. Sheridan knew there was nothing more she could ask Vida. The woman had given the best she could.

Vida smiled at Sheridan redirecting her friend's thoughts. "You know what? You should explore a meadow outside Hidden. You will love it. It will help you refocus."

"Wow that's a side step if I ever heard one. But, it seems that's the best offer I have been given so far." Sheridan waved her hand over her head making a whooshing sound. "Okay, one thing at a time here. I need to analyze what you just said. Then we can talk about pretty meadows." The researcher in Sheridan took over. "First you have all been holding back about Hidden. I'm asking why?"

"We are revealing Hidden a little at a time. We aren't holding back so much as we are teaching slowly. It's like one of your classes. You can't teach the end of the textbook first and expect your student to understand, right?"

Sheridan shook her head and gave a loud sigh. "Okay, so you are telling me that I am here to learn something about Hidden?"

"Yes, but also about yourself dear."

"Whew! I think I was better off in oblivion after I fainted." Sheridan's frustration was like an itch inside a wound. "Lets leave that for now and go on" Sheridan pursued Vida's lead. "You said Hidden is a place that is in between life and dream. So am I semi-comatose? Am I dead? How do I interpret that?"

Vida took Sheridan's hands in her own. "You are not asleep dear. You are very much alive. That probably wasn't the best analogy, but I simply don't know how else to say it."

"Why not just tell me where or what Hidden is?"

"Honey, it's like I just said about your college class. You have to explore and take the information in as you discover it."

"Okay," Sheridan threw her hands up in mock surrender letting out a long sigh. "That will have to do, at least for now. My mind isn't processing this information very well yet. You say there is a meadow I should see outside of town." Sheridan sighed in surrender.

"Oh yes, it is one of the most peaceful places. You will love it. I'm not going to tell any more because I want you to see for yourself." Vida became animated. "I've never seen a meadow quite like it. It's got a... woops," She put her hand over her mouth and chuckled. "I almost let something out of the bag."

"Vida, you are teasing me now. I can't resist a good puzzle." Sheridan's heavy sigh of exasperation gave her a steam vent for her smoldering agitation. "Okay, maybe the fresh air and a change of scene will do me good. Hidden is small enough to be almost claustrophobic."

Vida smiled. "You will go tomorrow. I'll fix a lunch and send you on your way. Although, there is enough fruit to eat, you probably won't eat the lunch. Catch said he gave you an old map. It should be on there, but it's not hard to find. Just follow the path out the other end of town."

Vida's enthusiasm was catching. "I'm actually feeling a whole lot better. Thank you Vida." Sheridan lied.

"That's a date then?"

"That's a date. Tomorrow about lunch time" Sheridan was feeling better after all.

Vida spat in her hand and held it out to Sheridan. "Come on, it's a promise."

Sheridan shook her head, spat in her own hand, and shook with Vida. Thank goodness, it was only a few wet sprinkles of saliva. Sheridan was ready to wash her hands. "I haven't done that since my sister and I were little." Sheridan said as she pulled a tissue from the box by the bed and wiped her hand. She handed a tissue to Vida.

"Ah, sometimes it's good to be a kid." Vida laughed. "As soon as I make you that sandwich, I'm Service again." Vida bounced off the bed and walked out of the room with an equally bouncy step. Sheridan chuckled. Then the questions, from which her mind had a temporary rest, came flooding back.

"Vida," Sheridan called after her friend. "I really am anxious to get back to Lincoln. Now that I've talked to Michael, I want to see my real home again. I know that isn't it beyond that door. I don't know how Catch, or whoever managed that stunt. I just want to go home."

Vida hurried back to Sheridan pulling her into a tight hug. "Well the way is blocked right now, but it may

open up soon. Shepherd will be here. I
know he's looking forward to seeing
you. He will be able to help you more."

"I keep hearing about this Shepherd.
Is he the mayor or something?"

"Yes, I guess he is kind of like a
mayor, and sheriff, and sage, and lots of
things. Oh, just wait until you meet him
Sheridan. You will find out he is the
very best of friends to have."

Vida's in love

Chapter 6: Tormented Dreams

Sheridan undressed and grabbed the silk nightgown and robe someone left on the bed when she wasn't looking. She didn't think she had worn any of her own nightclothes since her arrival.

Pulling her auburn locks up in a ponytail, she grabbed a towel and stepped into the sauna inside the sinfully huge bathroom. Sheridan spread dipper after dipper over the hot coals until the steam was so dense, she couldn't see her own hand more than a few inches in front of her face. The heat warmed her skin opening the pores as sweat dripped from her body.

Sheridan reluctantly left the sauna's relaxing heat letting a plume of steam into the cooler air of the room.

The shower was equally welcome as the massaging heads pelted her tense muscles. After which she finally wiped the steam from the mirrors and dried off her slim frame. She stood in front of the mirror running her hands over her perky breasts. She was finally satisfied there were no

lumps and she finished her bathing routine, then donned the gown and robe.

She sat on the lounger sofa in her room and ate the nuts and fruit from the bowl on the table. Weary and full, the bed seemed to swaddle her and she fell into a deep slumber.

"Sheridan, it's mommy, you need to wake up now. Your appendix is all gone."

"She's going to be a little groggy for a while and we'll be giving her pain medicine that will make her a little woozy. She should be waking up very soon. She may not remember much tomorrow. She'll be like a drunken child today." A nasal voice spoke over the child in the hospital white bed.

"Thank you nurse, Sheridan has always been independent and active. It's a little disturbing to see her lay here all pale. I always did like to watch her sleep, though she didn't know it. I always used to set the Lunis Flower by her bedside. She loves the Lunis Flower."

"What Lunis Flower mother? I don't remember any flower at all." Sheridan heard herself saying in the corner of the room looking on as if she wasn't the child at all.

"Let me up, let me up." The little girl demanded weakly, her voice hoarse and raspy. "Mommy, make them let me go, I will be late."

The adult Sheridan in the corner watched as the nurse held the shoulders of the child.

"Late for what honey?" mother asked.

"Mommy, don't be so silly. I'm going to be late for school. Let me uh-uh-up." The young reddish brown haired girl whined. Her little voice squeaked in protest.

Sheridan hovered in the corner wanting to sooth the child, the child that had been her. The mother turned her face toward the clock on the wall where Sheridan floated. Sheridan was looking directly into her mother's face.

There was laughter in the distance. The little girl coughed sending a shock of pain from her abdomen across her back.

Sheridan wondered why she felt the pain the child was feeling. She looked down to see herself in a small hospital gown with a pooch on her right side where a large bandage covered her wound.

"I'm sorry honey." Sheridan felt someone press something soft against her stomach. "Cough again honey, it will help you get rid of that old anesthesia."

Everything the child did, the grown Sheridan did in unison. Small Sheridan cried for her mother. "Mommy, I want the Lunis Flower."

Instantly something changed. She wasn't in the hospital now. She heard someone in her room. Footsteps softly swept across her floor and she screamed for her mother to save her. "Shh, you're okay."

The image of her mother disappeared.

She must have quieted for a while, because at the next moment a man with a machine gun was riding past her yelping at the top register of his voice.

She was an adult in this scene. The man's horse ran directly at her, knocked her off her feet with its flank, and galloped on. The man threw something with a flame into a hole in the desert ground.

Then she saw the man on the horse and it was Mark. She jumped back falling onto the sand and then saw herself as though outside of her body again. She flew into the hallway of the inn just outside her door where the balsa plaque hung. The symbols spelled something she couldn't quite

read, they kept twisting around themselves until they formed a name, but she couldn't read it. She reached out as if to catch the spinning balsa wood symbols and the dream ended.

Sheridan awoke sitting up in bed. Her body was wet with her own sweat. She reached down and grabbed her abdomen. The well-healed scar was still where it had been, but something else seemed hollow in her belly. Then she remembered the child she'd lost. Why had she dreamed the man who caused her husband Mark's death and the loss of her child was Mark himself?

Had she somehow blamed him all these years? It was from a memory buried in time, and now it surfaced to torment her once again.

Sheridan was glad to be awake and in a friendly bed. Memories could be painful, but this wasn't memory, it was torment. She pushed it from her mind.

"Today I am in Hidden, away from the trauma of that time. I have things to explore." She ran through the list of the present. She did the exercise when her anxiety and posttraumatic stress disorder tried to grasp her thoughts again.

A loud racket outside her room disrupted her thoughts. She heard Catch whisper to someone to be more quiet. Looking out the window, Sheridan realized it was still night. Now what, she asked herself. I'm wide-awake, but when she lay back on her pillow, it wasn't long until she was slumbering quietly. No more dreams or noises bothered her that night.

Waking up the next morning was a relief. The night riddled with dreams began to disconnect from the waking events of the night. She remembered the dreams vividly. She'd heard that dreams often helped to deal with things that people couldn't, or didn't want to deal with consciously. History was full of interpreters of dreams and their meanings. She didn't want to try to interpret that night's horrifying images. She wanted to rid herself of them for good.

Daylight poured through the window and a breeze blew softly through a sliver of open space deliberately measured for just the right amount of air movement.

Catch had visited her room again.

Such intrusions no longer bothered the young woman. However, when she swung her legs over the bedside, she noticed a crystal bud vase next to her bed on the table. The vase held an odd flower. It was the Lunis Flower.

She reached over and touched it. How soft and breathtaking it was.

The ivory colored, feathery petals were so delicate and strong under her touch. They were soft with a silky smoothness. The golden stamen looked unfinished. It wasn't quite mature enough to let go of its pollens. Oh, but how beautiful the color, it almost radiated its golden hue, but only almost.

She grasped the stem very lightly between her fingers so she could twirl it. It was strong for a flower stem, especially for such a delicate flower. It was like a rose stem without the thorns.

Then she brushed the leaf with the side of her finger. It was thick. Its heart shape had red veins following the center from where it attached to the stem. It didn't seem fully-grown, but Sheridan could not have said why.

Bringing it to her nose, the fragrance of the Lunis flower was like new life. The smell of a baby came to mind. It was not an overpowering smell at all. It was like a scented soap, clean and untouched. It was so close to perfect,
she knew why nobody had captured it's essence in any art form.

She carefully slipped the flower back into the small vase. Her heart raced as if parting with it brought the reality of its presence to the front of her consciousness. How had the dream flower become real? Catch must have brought it in when he came in to open the window. That opened yet another question: Why was he so secretive about its location? Where did he get it?

Sheridan let out a deep sigh, then got up and dressed for the day. Today she would explore the meadow. After she confronted Catch about the disturbance during the night. Although, she thought, thankfully, she woke to a refreshing breeze and the gift of the Lunis flower. She should thank him for that.

Catch was such a contradiction. Even his hands seemed to have more significance. She felt there was a reason one was a child's hand and the other a man. It was more than a birth defect. She'd seen him work with both, noticing how they almost worked without the knowledge of the other. It was as if they moved like the tentacles of an octopus.

What should she say? How could she tell him she didn't like him going in and out of her room, but still tell him how thankful she was for the amazing gift? She didn't want to send a mixed message to him.

Sheridan brushed the curtain back hoping the door would be gone to the replica of her house. To her surprise, it was there, unlocked and easily opened.

She looked into her home from Lincoln, exactly as it had been when Catch first directed her to it. She didn't dare close the door for it may disappear.

She reached behind her and opened the door into the Inn's hallway. Sheridan backed quickly through it afraid something else would change if she didn't monitor it. As she closed the door in front of her, she turned reluctantly away from it and moved forward.

With her large, loom woven shoulder tote held over her back with two fingers, she approached the ornate staircase to the lobby. Two male voices caught her interest as she descended.

Chapter 7: Diggory

"Good morning Sheridan, we have a new arrival to keep you company. This is Diggory. You two have something in common. You are both looking for something. His name means "lost one"." Catch chuckled to himself.

"Hello Diggory," she extended a hand. He took it but his handshake was clammy and weak. She sensed the uncertainty in the young man. "Don't worry Diggory; this town has a thing about name meanings. I think they must all take a course in it."

"Nice to meet you too, Sheridan. I - I guess the next thing is, what does your name mean?"

Before Sheridan could answer Catch piped up, "Sheridan is the searcher."

"Thanks for that Catch, but I do know what my name means."

Diggory looked to be about twenty, blonde wavy hair, green eyes, and a definite tan. His features were very pleasant and seemed almost carved straight from Michelangelo's David. Except if he was an image of David, he was an unhealthy one. His eyes gave away his sadness. They were glassy, with dilated pupils, and sunken. He had a tendency to scratch at the bend of his inner elbow through his shirt. Sheridan had little doubt that Diggory was a drug addict.

"How did you get here, Diggory?" Sheridan hesitated. The answer to that question could show the way out of the small unexplainable town.

"I'm not sure. There was a gas station, and then here. I think the station is down that road, but I don't know. There is a wild fire out there now."

Sheridan was out the door like a shot. She ran to the end of the only road in and out of Hidden. The way seemed clear enough. Without a thought, her legs carried her down the road until she reached the sign that struck her as ironic when she first found the small town. Any attempt to go beyond that sign induced coughing spasms from the irritating thick smoke.

The heat seared her flesh as soon as she attempted to push past the barrier. She stepped backward one-step away from the sign and the air was cool and clear, although she could see the smoke and dancing flames in front of her.

What if this is just a vision?
Sheridan thought. What if I could walk
right through it and find my way out?
However, every attempt to penetrate the
barrier issued the same result.

She turned back toward Hidden
feeling as if someone had just beaten her
into submission.

A wooden bench to the left of the
huge doors provided a spot to cry over
the frustration of no escape.

"Are you alright lady?" Diggory
stood beside the bench.

"What is this place? It's like a trap.
There is no way out except that road and
it's a one way trap." Sheridan spat the
word 'trap' as if it had a foul flavor.

"I'll get us out of here. Nobody is
going to trap me." Diggory ran up the

road. Within minutes, he returned coughing uncontrollably until he reached Street. His breathing cleared. "I don't like this place; it's like an alien world. Where are we?"

"I wish I knew." Sheridan's head dipped until it rested on her hands supported by her knees. "I'm supposed to go to a meadow that Vida told me about. Maybe there will be a way out there."

"I'm sorry." Diggory sat back down on the bench. "I didn't mean to yell at you. Who is Vida? Can I go to the meadow with you?"

"I know you didn't mean to yell at me. Vida is probably the best friend I've found here, but even she avoids answering my questions. She works at the café. By the way, when we're at the café, Vida insists on being called Service."

"That's weird. Who would want that?"

"I haven't the slightest idea. She told me it's because serving other's is what she loves about herself. Cook is quite a character as well."

Diggory laughed.

Sheridan suddenly realized how absorbed she was in her own problem.

"How about you Diggory, are you alright? If there was an explosion and you don't remember anything else, you may have a concussion."

"I don't feel bad at all. Far as I know, there's not a mark on me anywhere. I guess I just found my way here."

"You sure did. I don't know what gas station you were at, but the last gas stop was at least twenty miles east just this side of Omaha. If you were coming from Lincoln, it's about the same distance."

"I-80, I wasn't on I-80. I was on Highway 50 far south of I-80. I was heading for the interstate, but I don't remember getting that far."

"I think we need to ask some more questions." Sheridan said with determination. "I've had a lot of questions here, but few satisfactory answers, and a lot of very odd things going on. I have a feeling this place wouldn't show up on any road map."

You're making me nervous. I'm just a kid trying to get a car across country and collect my money. It's a two day job and I really need that money." The young man's voice wavered nervously.

"I'm sorry. I haven't even introduced myself properly and I'm throwing a fit about my own problems." Sheridan smiled at the young man. She felt a maternal attraction toward him. "Now that you are in Hidden, Diggory, you will find a lot of the residents very nice if a bit odd. Catch, I take him with a grain of salt. I'll introduce you to some of the other's later."

Sheridan tossed her hair and drew her hands down her face. "I just had a bad night last night."

Diggory started laughing wildly causing Sheridan too look up at him.

"You," he pointed to her face "You have a smudge of ash on your face. I don't think it's the right color for you."

"Oh my Lord," Sheridan laughed at herself. "I better wash up before I ask Catch anything. Can you imagine me trying to look serious with ash and soot all over me? Wait here, I'll be back after I clean up."

Diggory smiled. "It's just a small streak. I didn't even notice it until a minute ago."

"That's good; it must have been a piece of ash from the fire." Sheridan replied.

"Hey Sheridan," Diggory called after her when she got to the door. "I'm sorry if I woke you last night. Catch said he tried to quiet me down, but I was so high. I think I smoked a couple of joints and did some coke before I got here. I'm sorry about that."

"Well, if you were high, that might explain why you don't remember getting to I-80, or even to here. Hwy 50 does run into I-80 west of Omaha. If you turned west toward Lincoln, you may have come upon Hidden. Logically, that's most likely." Sheridan sighed sadly. "Son, I hope you can

get off that stuff. You will live a much better life without it."

"I know that. I think most of us on hard drugs do, but the drugs take over. Maybe if I'm here a while I'll get through the hard part. They seem to have been expecting me."

"How is that?"

"That old guy, Catch, took me to my room. It's all about my favorite stuff, like my poems catalogued in a scrapbook. I didn't even remember that I wrote enough to fill a scrapbook that big. The walls are painted with a mural of flame like on a racecar. It's amazing how they got it all together. There is a lot more too, but the weirdest thing is a picture of a flower they call the Lunis flower. I never was interested in flowers, but this one has something about it. I asked who came up with the idea for that one, and Catch said it's a real flower. Cool huh?"

Diggory didn't wait for Sheridan to answer as he continued with his fascination about the Inn, and especially with his room and Catch. "My favorite sports magazines were even there. That bathroom is better'n anything I've ever had before. I love the multiple showerheads. I swear, after my shower this morning, just about every muscle felt like butter." He laughed and Sheridan saw joy in his eyes. He took a deep breath. He didn't say anymore, but shrugged raising his arms up and letting them fall to his side.

Sheridan squelched the temptation to forewarn him to take caution with falling for the aesthetics and amenities. She wasn't sure about the reasoning behind all the seeming foreknowledge of the town's people not only of visitors' arrivals, but also of their lives. She thought it best to let him make up his own mind. She was sure it wasn't a retreat or rehabilitation resort.

She must have shaken her head to clear it. "Lady, I think you need to come back to earth as much as I do."

Sheridan smiled. "I'm sorry. Let's go back in, talk to Catch and ask him a couple of questions. Then if you don't care, I'll take you with me to the café if you like."

"That sounds good. I'm starving even though I had a bunch of that fruit this morning. Did they have a huge bowl of fruit in your room?"

"Yes, and it's refilled every day." She smiled at Diggory. To disturb his happiness would be wrong. Maybe his innocence about Hidden would carry him through his stay. He didn't seem in any hurry to go anywhere else.

"Catch?" Sheridan yelled when she didn't find him in the lobby or the room with all the memorabilia. He didn't answer and she didn't feel like chasing him down. After the night she'd had, and the morning's revelations, she didn't really want to deal with his head games.

"We'll talk to him later." Sheridan told Diggory. "Come on, let's go get a sandwich. Cook makes the best sandwiches I've ever tasted."

The two walked the short distance to the Hidden Café.

Sheridan guided Diggory to the same booth she usually sat at. It was in the middle along the wall in front of a leaded glass window that dispersed the light through the crystal version of the Lunis flower.

"Hey, they have the flower three dimensional here." His enthusiasm made Sheridan a little sad. She was happy for him, but it made her miss the energy and joy she'd felt when she was young, living simply in the Sahara desert with Mark. He seemed to be coming to mind a lot more since she'd landed in Hidden.

"Hi Sheridan and I believe you are Diggory. What are you hungry for?"

Vida's bright voice flew across the room. "I have sandwiches for all of us.

How about some coffee before we take off."

Sheridan looked at her puzzled. Then her eyes popped wider as she remembered the trip to the meadow that Vida planned for her. "The meadow, I forgot with all that's happened this morning."

Vida shook her head. "No matter, you're still here and I have stuff ready to go. What's more, I'm going with you both."

"Hi Diggory, I'm Service," Vida changed to her café identity and sat across from the two as Cook brought four teacups and a carafe on a silver tray. He set it in the middle of the table.

"This is Cook." Sheridan introduced the smiling man with the white apron.

"Wow, I don't think I've had tea from a tea set since I was a little girl."

"Well then, it's time you did." Cook observed in his full baritone.

Diggory whispered, "My grandmother served tea every day from a tea service just like that one. It even had the mismatched cup. That cup was mine; she said it made me extra special and unique." His voice quivered.

Sheridan looked at him and saw the tears running down his face unchecked. "Where did you get that set?"

Neither Cook nor Service answered. Service poured out the tea handing the mismatched cup to Diggory.

"You deserve to drink from that cup again, Diggory." Service said almost like a prayer. "You are special and very unique."

"I'm a damned useless addict." He almost spat his self-hatred, pulling his arms back above his head as if touching the cup might somehow burn him.

"No, Diggory, you are a wonderful young man who lost his way for a little bit. You are certainly not useless." Service injected.

The young man carefully picked up the cup. He took a sip of the ginger flavored tea with one cube of sugar. "That's even the kind of tea she served. She was British and never lost that part of her heritage. She didn't immigrate until after my parents died. Then she died last year."

Nobody said anything as Cook put the set on a table close by. Service put her hand palm down in the middle of the table nodding at the others to do the same. Cook and Sheridan put their hands on top of hers and finally Diggory placed his hand atop the pile.

"To the meadow," Cook announced and the four raised their hands. "To the meadow," they repeated.

Chapter 8: The Meadow

As they left the café, Diggory walked along behind them. Sheridan looked back and he seemed to be with them only in body. "Diggory, are you with us?"

His head popped up. "Who are you people? What is happening here? This is all too much and I think I've just woke up to what is really going on here. Sheridan, now I know why you wanted out of here so bad. It's weird, Twilight Zone weird."

Sheridan dropped back to walk with him, letting Cook and Vida walk ahead a few steps.

His outburst was unexpected, but Sheridan felt it was far overdue. "I felt the same way Diggory. It's very confusing. It's too weird. I keep hoping Vida's friend Shepherd will tell us when he gets here. Believe me, I've asked questions but nobody gives a complete answer."

Vida and Cook didn't respond at all. It was as if they hadn't even heard. Sheridan trusted Vida most of all, but her all too frequent lack of response made Sheridan question that trust.

"I love it down in here." Vida's breathy coo was almost like a fresh breeze.

"My lord," Sheridan spoke her thoughts aloud. "I just realized its still morning."

Then she spoke loudly enough for Vida and Cook to hear. "Did you hear Diggory?"

"Yes, we heard him." Cook spoke
first.

"He needed to vent." Vida followed.
"We didn't feel the need to say anything
else, especially so close to the meadow.
You will both feel better there."

"See what I mean?" Sheridan
whispered to Diggory.

They all stepped onto the dirt path
leading to what Sheridan expected to be
like any other clearing in a Nebraska
pasture. They walked over a small rise
that looked down on a huge meadow.
Just below the top of that rise were rows
of wild flowers.

"Wow, there are so many of them.
Did you raise these Vida? They look like
they grow in a spiral. What are they?
Are any of them Lunis Flowers?"

"Take a breath Sheridan" Vida laughed. "I've never seen any Lunis Flower here, have you Cook?"

Cook shook his head.

"No, Sheridan, I didn't plant any of it. It's a natural border. Lift your eyes and look at the way the flowers swirl around the area until they meet the tree line. How they came to grow like this, I have no idea. It's like a beautiful painting of swirling color. Here and there, the colors merge."

The four people stood side-by-side looking down on the multitude of colors, intermingled like pixels on a screen, blending almost into a picture.

They all breathed in the scented mixture on the breeze. "There, I see one. It looks just like the one Catch placed by my bed."

"Sheridan stop" Vida yelled.

"Why? I just want to pick one."

"It's not a Lunis Flower Sheridan. It's one of those things of nature that imitates the real thing and then it burns you."

"What are you talking about? I held the one in my room this morning. It never hurt me at all."

Vida held her hand out in front of her motioning for Sheridan to stop. Each time Sheridan would move as if to pick the flower, Vida repeated the motion.

Cook walked toward Sheridan and took hold of her hands.

"The one you saw this morning didn't have any of the sap still coming out of the stem did it?" Cook asked.

"Well, no it was in water and had probably been picked for a little while." Sheridan said. "I understand if you didn't plant any Lunis Flowers here Vida, but this really looks just like the ones I've seen."

"Sheridan, you've never seen the real Lunis Flower, you have seen a painting, crystal imitation, and a few other attempts at reproducing its image." Vida said sweetly. "In the painting, what color were the petals?"

"They were white. It was as if the artist was trying to capture the whitest white possible." Sheridan looked back to see the flower she'd almost picked. "That has ivory petals. You mean the real one does have white petals? I'm glad you stopped me. Is it some sort of nettle or something?"

"It feels a lot like a nettle if you get any of that sap on you." Vida answered.

"Hoorah, Sheridan. Vida just gave you a complete answer to a question. She gave you a whole lot of answers." Diggory made himself known.

Sheridan laughed, "Yes she did, Diggory. Thank you Vida."

Diggory shook his head as if Sheridan hadn't caught the sarcasm in his voice. But, she not only caught it, she was irritated at Diggory for it. Vida and Cook kept her from getting a nasty, burning rash. She didn't feel sarcasm was appropriate. "Well everyone let's go. I'm anxious to see that meadow."

Sheridan took a deep breath and exhaled all the tension of the moments before. She opened her eyes and looked down the path toward the tree line.

Sheridan gasped letting her eyes follow the floral pinwheel. "It's like layered rainbows. I could never snap a photograph that would capture this. There is nothing wrong with any of these other flowers?"

"Nope," Vida said brightly.

Sheridan stooped over, picked a petal from a wild rose, and laid it on her tongue. Closing her mouth onto the petal, she sniffed the air again to enhance the dusty, sweet flavor.

"I can't believe you just did that." Vida chuckled.

Sheridan's three companions were looking at her. "You've never heard of eating a rose? Cook surely you have."

"Well, yes," he said, "but I've never actually done it."

Sheridan snickered. "I just had to for some reason. I've eaten one before, and it's kind of a dusty, sweet taste. I don't know how else to explain it. It's not something I'd put on my salads, but the taste of that rose petal, with the fresh air, filled with all these wonderful smells, makes me feel like I belong to this place."

"That's a change." Diggory said as if betrayed. "Thanks a lot Sheridan. I like flowers, but I've never seen one that could make me change my mind that quick. Not even a poppy."

"Oh Diggory, I'm not forgetting anything, I'm just happy for some reason."

"You are a romantic, Sheridan Easterly." Vida accused.

"Yup, and you Vida, are no longer looking like you want to clobber someone." Sheridan smiled. "Come on Vida give it a try."

Vida wrinkled up her nose, but Sheridan convinced her to taste a rose petal. "Well, I see a little of what you mean. I guess I don't have the perspective that you have. It's okay, but Sheridan I'm sorry, I just don't get a thrill from it, that's for sure." Vida refused to swallow the flower petal but delicately pulled it out of her mouth and threw it away.

Sheridan laughed, "Okay Vida, if I'm the romantic, you're the pragmatic."

"I'm with Vida." Cook spoke up.

"Me too," Diggory agreed.

Vida smiled and changed the subject. "See that tree line ahead?" She pointed. "We get through there and we are in the meadow. Let's go, I'm getting hungry."

"So the rose wasn't such a bad appetizer after all." Sheridan teased.

Sheridan paid little attention to the trees until Vida mentioned them. She had thought they were already in the meadow. Once they passed the first tree, the land lay out flat before them. It looked like a carpet of greenery.

It was full of ferns and bluegrass that nature had sculpted into the beautiful landscape. They could see at least a mile or more ahead. Some trees dotted here and there full of fruits and nuts of all kinds. It seemed they were in a greenhouse of fruit trees of every kind in the world. There were apple, pear, peach, walnut, pecan, pomegranate, fig, olive, cherry, and more.

Vida pulled a ripe pear off a nearby branch and bit into it. "Go ahead, there's a lot to choose from. What is your favorite?"

Sheridan reached for a peach. The flavor of the meat of the fruit beyond its furry skin tasted sweet and juicy. She grabbed a pear from the tree Vida had picked from and took a bite of the firm, gritty fruit. "There isn't a blemish on any of it. This is heaven Vida. Isn't it?" Diggory and Cook were eating apples.

Both looked up when they heard
Sheridan's question.

"I think it's pretty close to heaven.
Look, Sheridan, all of this, not one thing
has disturbed this meadow. Even the
path doesn't go past the trees."

"What about animals? There have to
be animals."

"Oh yes. There are a lot of them.
They're out there if you look."

Sheridan plucked a fresh
pomegranate. The burst of flavor from
the hard, nutty granules inside the fruit
surprised her. A fresh purple plum
sharpened the tongue with it's not quite
ripe tartness. She looked at the others
and noticed they too were eating from
several trees.

"Are you ready for sandwiches?" Vida asked.

"No," the other three said in unison as they patted their full tummies.

"Thought so," Vida teased. "That's why I never packed any." She laughed and her laugh was so infectious even Diggory joined in the mirth.

Beep, Beep, the noise shocked both Sheridan and Diggory, but it didn't seem to faze their other two companions.

Cook pulled a cellular phone from an apron pocket. He listened for a moment. "Great, we'll be there."

His excitement was taken up by Vida who cut in, "It's time, and he's coming?"

"He sure is coming. We better go get ready for him."

"What is this?" Diggory was obviously angry, and Sheridan was feeling betrayed as well. "You have had a cell phone this whole time?"

Sheridan looked at Diggory whose face was red and puffed out with his anger. She was afraid he would hit Cook, so she stepped in between the two and tried to calm him down.

"Hey," she said calmly placing her hands on both of Diggory's cheeks. "I know how you feel. I'm angry to, but please don't start hitting. I couldn't stand it." Sheridan's intense pleas surprised even her. It was then she realized just how much the violence of her past affected her. "Please, Diggory."

"I won't hit him, but I do want answers." Diggory's clenched his teeth tightly around the words.

"We haven't deceived you two. We have a single cell phone that only works between here and Hidden. We are otherwise in a dead zone. It would have been of no use to either of you to call home or anywhere. If we'd gone past the meadow, it would not work there either."

"I'm sorry we didn't let you know about it earlier. It didn't occur to us." Vida's apology sounded sincere.

"It took us off guard. Please don't be lying to us about this." Sheridan stopped speaking suddenly. "Catch tricked me about the call to my home? How would he be able to do that?"

Vida held the phone out to Sheridan who took it and dialed her home phone number. There was nothing, not even a single bar indicating a signal. All she heard was dead space.

"I am being truthful with you Sheridan." Vida reassured her friend as she took the cell phone back. "Now we have to go and get ready for Shepherd. He is coming back and he will explain all of this to you. Everything is going to become clear to you. Just have a little more faith in us. Please!"

Vida seemed to have complete faith in Shepherd. Sheridan hoped he was worth it. What puzzled Sheridan was that Cook was as excited as Vida was about Shepherd's arrival.

"You two keep exploring the meadow. Please enjoy yourselves. I think you will find your way back easily as long as you start back before dark. There is only one path for you to take."

Cook said as the two quickly walked back toward Hidden.

Chapter 9: The Lake

"Well, I guess that's that. They have decided the order of our day for us." Diggory said with more than a hint of sarcasm.

"Well, I'm kind of glad Diggory. Can I just call you Dig? You can call me Sher. It's a nickname I'm used to."

"Yea, almost everyone I know calls me Dig. It's kind of funny because I'm one of those who likes to dig into a subject or event and get down to the nitty gritty of it, no matter what that may be."

"Well, that's something we have in common. I'm an anthropologist."

"Really, I was working on my required courses, but my plan was to become a geologist."

"Who says you have to give that up. Get rid of the past tense Dig."

"I don't know if I'm confident enough for that yet, but I'll check out the geography of this place with you. It looks out of this world."

"Ha, Ha, Dig, were you raised in a hippy commune?"

"How did you know?"

Sheridan laughed louder. However mixed up and lost Diggory was, for the moment he made her forget her own problems.

"It must be some botanical experiment, but I can't quite figure out how they perfected the climate."

Diggory's observation took Sheridan off guard. "What?"

"Well, look at this meadow. Where on Earth would you find this variety of vegetation? And..." Diggory sucked in a deep breath. He pointed at the reason for his shock.

Sheridan followed his direction and gasped as well.

"I've never ever heard of a black bear lying beside a donkey like that. My God Sheridan, this has to be one of the best-kept secrets ever. That is impossible, but there it is."

"There must be some kind of explanation. Maybe it's a preserve and the animals were born and raised here?"

"How does that explain a climate that would allow them to grow this variety of fruits and nuts?"

"This meadow is a garden. It's not just a meadow. I think we have found our way into some odd scientific experiment."

"So, you think maybe they are using us as a part of it? Like, maybe they want to see how humans of today would respond to something like that." Diggory pointed to the bear and donkey joined by a deer.

"Well, the deer makes sense in Nebraska." Sheridan observed.

"Maybe the area comes with the climate, or at least was easy to put in some kind of artificial climate controlled force field." Diggory proposed the idea.

"Oh, now you are getting weird on me."

"No," he said. "It's a real possibility. Things exist that we know nothing about. The authorities keep them confidential. But, I have heard that force fields and climate control of an area are closer to possible than any of us think." He looked down at Sheridan. "I watch a lot of educational television."

Sheridan was giving what he said some serious thought. "So they would be creating a huge, climate controlled, Garden of Eden?"

"Yes, in a manner of speaking, that would be the optimal result."

"Wow!" Sheridan started walking toward the lake.

"Careful"

"I'm taking it slow. I don't feel like I'm in any danger." Sheridan continued toward the body of water. Diggory walked in a sideways at-the-ready posture beside her until they reached the water's edge.

They left a 100-foot space between them and the animals, who didn't stir.

The lake was clear as glass. Sitting on smooth flat rocks, they peered into the clean water and dipped their hands in it for a refreshing drink. Without speaking, they realized something in the water changed them in some subtle way. They took another drink and healing seemed to build up in them giving them renewed vigor.

Sheridan looked at her young companion. "Diggory, you look healthy. I mean, when you got here your eyes looked sunken, you were thin, unkempt, and to tell the truth reeked of marijuana." She paused. "I'm sorry, that wasn't nice. The point is you are completely changed. I noticed some changes after you ate the fruit and nuts. You seem to have a little more color in your cheeks. But, now" she paused, "your face is filled out and you have a healthy glow."

"I think I should say thank you," Diggory teased. "Don't worry about it. I know what you mean. Just one thing, you didn't say if I smell better."

They both chuckled and Sheridan expanded. "Well, you smell fresh, like a new born baby, how about me?"

"Hmm, well you smell nice, maybe like a baby."

"You're flirting," Sheridan accused.

"Shamelessly," Diggory admitted. "Anyway, you look beautiful. Now that I look at you with new eyes, you look tons younger. I'd say you look about twenty-five. All of your care lines are gone. You don't have one wrinkle or line by your eyes. Did you have a facelift within the last five minutes?"

Sheridan looked into the lake, which was so clear the pebbles and small fish at the bottom of the lake broke her reflection. "I think I can almost see what you are saying." Sheridan turned her face trying to catch a better reflection.

Diggory started laughing and pushed on her arm. "You are making funny faces. Didn't you know your face could stick like that?" He was laughing hard and holding his stomach.

"Oh, ha ha," Sheridan retorted with a mock giggle. "The lake must be fed by a mineral spring." She looked at Diggory's long sleeves covering his arms. "Take off your shirt."

"What? Now who's flirting?"

"No, Diggory, I'm being clinical. I know why you are hiding your arms. I've seen you rubbing them through your sleeves. I want to see if the healing properties of the water help with your wounds." Sheridan was careful not to call the 'wounds' needle track marks.

"Yeah, I guess it's hard to fool someone as observant as you." He took off his shirt.

Sheridan gasped at the hideous sight of the infected injection sites not only inside his elbows, but also on his stomach and on his neck below the collar. "Sorry Diggory, I didn't expect..."

"You didn't expect it to be this bad. Sheridan I'm a junkie. We don't care about our bodies, or anything but the next fix. I've shot up with a lot of stuff and inhaled nearly anything that gives a high. I've stolen, beaten

people up for what few coins I could get off them. If you can imagine any horrific thing a person can do, it's likely I've done it."

"Okay, I was just shocked. I want to wet your shirt in the water and wipe your wounds. Some of them look very infected." Sheridan rinsed his shirt several times before wringing it and wiping Diggory's wounds. The healing was instantaneous. The infection disappeared. There wasn't even a scar left over from the fiery red sores.

The two looked at each other with their mouths wide open, eyes big as plates. Sheridan wet the shirt again and washed the sores on his abdomen with the same result. "This can't be. I - I - ah, what are we supposed to think about this Diggory?"

"You've got me. I mean, it's great to see my sores gone, but this is weird."

"Dig, this is more than weird. It's miraculous."

Diggory jumped to his feet and ran toward the far edge of the clearing.

"Where are you going?" Sheridan took off after him, surprised at how young and healthy she felt. She hadn't been able to run that well for probably twenty years.

"I'm going to see what's past these trees." Diggory yelled back. When they reached the tree line, neither of them was out of breath. "Did we just discover the fountain of youth?" Sheridan asked rhetorically.

There was a well-tended row of grapes nearby. Each grabbed a cluster of the juicy, purple grapes. "Mmm, these are delicious." Sheridan's blue eyes rolled with pleasure.

Diggory was pulling back the thick foliage and peering through the trees when Sheridan started to follow him. She could see the path was much darker and smelled a musty, sour odor when

Diggory turned grabbing her shoulders and pushed her back. "We aren't going in there. We'd be lost or

dead within minutes."

"Oh, you are exaggerating Dig, just a little aren't you?"

"Not even a little bit."

"We need to get back before dark anyway. Come on, I have some questions to ask. I'm tired of this so good, so bad crap." She took off at a run back toward town.

"Hold on there lady." Diggory called. "I've got some questions of my own."

When they arrived back at Hide Inn, it was dusk.

Sheridan stepped heavily through the hall and into the lobby yelling, "Catch" the whole way.

"What is going on here?" The old bearded innkeeper came around a corner with part of his supper still on his moustache. The fact that whatever it was looked bloody was not something Sheridan wanted to see right then.

"Catch, where are we? What is this place?"

"Umm, Hidden, standing in the middle of my inn shouting at me like a crazy woman."

"That's not what I mean and I think you know it. What is this place? There doesn't seem to be a way out once you get in. We just came from the most life-sustaining ecosystem I've ever seen. That meadow has fruit and nut trees, plants and animals anyone could ever want to see. It is idyllic. We just drank from that lake and both of us are healthier than we've probably ever been and when I washed Diggory's sores they not only healed they disappeared." Sheridan stopped for a breath after her rant.

Catch was looking at them as if he was waiting for the complaint. "Uh, so what is the problem?"

"It's unnatural." Diggory jumped in. "Then I looked through the trees and past them I see a dark canyon full of, I don't know what I saw, but it had the most awful stench."

"You went into the canyon? How did you get back out of it?" Catch looked surprised.

"Don't be evasive." Diggory spoke up. "I didn't say we went into it. I saw it. I stopped Sheridan and we high tailed it out of there."

"Okay," Catch looked almost ill. "I wanted to wait until you felt comfortable living with me before I said anything." Catch started to explain.

"Catch," a male voice came from behind them. Sheridan and Diggory turned in unison to see a man standing in front of them with loose fitting linen pants and tunic. He wore a woolen vest over his tan clothing.

"Who are you?" Diggory took the lead.

"I'm Shepherd." The man said simply as he opened the Shepherd's Closet door, put a long stick he held into a corner and hung his wool vest on a hook.

"Come little ones." Shepherd commanded and two sheep followed him outside.

Sheridan looked back at Catch. "Well, now that's another new one! So, that is Shepherd." She pointed toward the door where Shepherd disappeared a moment before. "Shepherd is a shepherd. Why would I have expected anything else in Hidden?"

Catch seemed nervous. "Would the two of you like to step out into my garden? It is very nice and Shepherd will be there later if you go there."

The old man's sudden agitation and offer confused Sheridan. "What garden? You've never mentioned it before.

Unless you mean the meadow, but we were there all day."

"No, there is a garden beyond the inn, through those doors."

They were standing in a ballroom in the opposite wing as the one Sheridan had seen before with all the pieces of people's lives.

They stood in a beautifully decorated room with red, velvet-upholstered gothic furniture made of dark walnut. There were side tables along the walls filled with vases of the imitation Lunis flowers.

The flowers, like the one in her room that morning were not quite right. The petals were every bit as feathery, but they were a very pale ivory, instead of the white of the ones in the pictures. The yellow stamen was just yellow, not the shimmering golden tones she'd seen portrayed, the leaves didn't seem as meaty, and the veins were thinner and not as red.

Nevertheless, Sheridan could barely believe they were as toxic as Cook and Vida led her to believe.

"That sounds nice Catch and if it's anywhere near as gorgeous as this room, I'm sure it would be pleasant. But, we came back for answers."

Diggory shook his head no. "I'm exhausted, and frustrated as hell. I think I'll go to my room and simmer down before bed. Enjoy a nice peaceful evening in your garden Catch."

"Oh, I don't go into the garden." Catch's shoulders slumped and he stood shuffling his feet. It was a long slide down his mountainous ego. Sheridan was puzzled and a little sorry for the old man. He suddenly had the ancient look of their first meeting.

Catch scratched his head. "Listen; and I mean listen carefully to what I say. You don't leave Hidden just because you want to. Hidden is not of the realm from whence you came. There are two destinations from here. It is totally up to you which way you go."

The soft but authoritative quality of Catch's voice caught them both off guard. Suddenly, Sheridan became very concerned about who the inhabitants of Hidden were and what they wanted from their guests.

"Are we prisoners then?" The threatening male voice came back. She knew Diggory angered easily.

"Not in the sense that you think sir. It will come clear to you as you pass through Hidden and the lands around it. Each leads to a new destination, but the choice will be yours. I must ask you a question now."

A dead calm came over the group. The deafening silence made Sheridan edgy and ready to snap at the old man. "What?" She flailed her arms in front of her. It was an impatient gesture, as was her tone.

"Do you believe me? It is very important that you believe what I tell you."

"After all that's happened, it's hard to trust anyone. But for now I'll believe you Catch." Sheridan replied.

"I'm not so sure you should Sheridan; don't be so easily taken in.

There is something going on here more than what he is telling us." Diggory said with his jaw clenched.

"Of course there is more than I have told you. You can't understand it all in one day or even in two or three."

"I want to see these other destinations so I can find a way to get the hell out of here?"

"Diggory," Catch tried to reason with the young man "You will see what is here for you to see. But, please keep an open mind."

Sheridan threw her hands out to her sides and let them flop back against her legs. With a huge sigh, she waved to Diggory and went to her rooms.

She didn't get any answers that night. She didn't feel it mattered anymore. Instead, she slipped into her home. She didn't think about it as a replica.

She wanted to feel familiarity. After making a small supper of a ham and cheese sandwich and some carrots, she sat down to eat behind the television. It didn't even occur to Sheridan that she was watching a news broadcast from Lincoln, NE.

Chapter 10: A Bit of Truth

Sheridan woke up in her own bed, in her own room, and in her own house.

A long stretch relieved her muscles of their morning stiffness. She wondered if Michael might come over, and then she remembered Vida, Catch, Diggory, and Cook.

She also remembered some faint figure called Shepherd.

Maybe sleeping here wasn't such a great idea after all.

The night's sleep remained uninterrupted with tormenting dreams. Breakfast was a delicious bagel with cream cheese. She found sliced strawberries in the refrigerator and placed them atop the cream cheese.

Sheridan had to admit Hidden's supplier knew quality and

was willing to pay the price for it. She enjoyed the pampering.

A sense of purpose behind the treatment she'd received tugged at her and made her wary, but she couldn't figure out what it was.

None of what she'd experienced was accidental. Even finding her way into the town days before must have been a part of their agenda. She just couldn't see how such a manipulation of events was possible.

The lobby of the inn was strangely empty. She found Hidden's population gathered in the large ballroom. Diggory came up behind her and stood at her side hooking his arm through hers. His action felt like a child seeking security. "What's this?"

"I don't know Dig. I just found everyone in there. It looks like Shepherd is speaking to them, but I can't hear any of it." Turning around she smiled up at her new friend. "The mute button got pushed I guess. Can you hear?"

Diggory snickered at her reference, "no. More secrets Sheridan, this is scaring me more every day. It's just not realistic."

Shepherd looked up and motioned the two into the room. "Please sit here at the front. I am ready to tell you some truth."

"That would be nice." Sheridan replied sarcastically.

"You have met everyone in Hidden. I want to let you know they are here for you. Each has had a part in your journey thus far."

"So, there is an agenda here? Why has no one answered our questions?" Sheridan asked.

"My beloved helpers in Hidden are not able to answer some questions without me. They are my liaisons."

"Liaisons after all this time and confusion, we find out that we have been held here by go betweens?" Diggory's voice rose to a crescendo.

"Vida, why didn't you tell me about this? You've been my closest friend since I've been here. Why couldn't you give me some idea? What is so special about this man that you all follow like those two sheep he brought in here last night?" Sheridan felt the hot tears of frustration flowing down her cheeks. "I was waiting for some big event. This is all there is?" Sheridan pointed to Shepherd.

"We help you while you are here. We are your connection until you find your way. Shepherd is much more than you see Sheridan. Please believe me, we told you all that we could. We don't go beyond the meadow." Vida pled with Sheridan.

Sheridan turned to Catch, who stood silently behind Shepherd. "Catch, what were you talking about last night? You said a lot I don't understand and I'm sure Diggory doesn't either. What did you mean by Hidden being of a different realm?"

Catch said nothing, he simply pointed to Shepherd.

"E-e-nough" Diggory yelled. "You're running some sort of cult, and pulled us into it. Ha, if you think you aren't going to let us go, I have news for you. I'm not asking permission." Diggory went on, "I'm getting out right now and I'm taking the lady with me."

Diggory's threatening tone didn't faze Shepherd. "Your stay in Hidden has been in preparation for the journey we are about to embark on. You have already tried to leave by the road, but you know you cannot go that way. You must follow me for now Diggory, or you will stay stranded where you are. What is your decision?"

"Huh," Diggory looked at Shepherd as though the other man was talking in riddles. "Didn't you hear me? I'm taking Sheridan out of this place. We'll get back to I-80 somehow if we cut through the trees. It can't be that far."

"You may try, but I believe Sheridan may wish to make up her own mind." Shepherd's voice never rose in anger or disgust. Sheridan understood Diggory's feelings and even agreed with him to a point, but she wasn't ready to leave without finding more about the journey ahead that Shepherd planned. If following Shepherd helped her get our of Hidden and home, she would definitely follow him.

"Diggory, I want to go with Shepherd. I must see this through. I don't know why, but I trust what he says. I think it will be okay."

Shepherd, a man of average height, dark olive skin, and no specially endearing features seemed to be in charge of everything. The word princely came to Sheridan's mind, even though outwardly, there was nothing striking about the man.

"Are we ready to go to the mountain?" Shepherd asked ignoring Diggory's hostility.

Sheridan had to admit when her travel companion mentioned the idea of a cult, memories of news reports about cults vowing to die with their leader flashed through her mind.

Shepherd spoke to them after having dismissed the town's people. "Sheridan, I know you are afraid and I understand why. I will lead you through much, both good and bad, but you will find wonderful answers."

He sat on a chair next to Diggory and spoke in a soothing voice as he would one of his sheep. "Diggory,"

Shepherd continued. "I know your life has been hard, but you are with me and I promise in time you will find all the assurance you could want. You are not wrong to question. It is a good thing. I will regain your trust if you follow me."

Diggory stiffened and jumped to his feet. "What? I have no idea who you are, how could I have ever put trust in you? What are you telling Sheridan, that you won't kill her, rape her, why should we go anywhere with you?"

"I understand your suspicions Diggory. Follow me and you will have your answers. We have a long journey ahead and we do not need to take anything because we will find all that we need along the way." Shepherd chuckled when he looked into Diggory's eyes, which were round and his mouth wide open as if in shock. "We are not a survivalist group either, Diggory, although you will survive only because you are with me."

"How would you know about my life?"

Shepherd pointed to the chairs in the ballroom. "The ones who sat in these chairs are very good listeners. They are also very observant."

"Should I go change my clothes and shoes?" Sheridan asked.

"Yeah, she can hardly go climbing in those thin canvas shoes she's wearing." Diggory defended Sheridan.

Shepherd looked down at his own feet and smiled. They were bare.

Sheridan loved a challenge. "Shepherd, what happened to the shoes you had on earlier?"

"I only wear those inside to keep the dirt from my feet from getting on the carpet."

Sheridan laughed. "That's kind of backward. I'll be fine in my thin canvas shoes, Dig."

Shepherd smiled, but gave no explanation as to why he wore shoes inside and not outside.

The trio walked out the large doors of the inn with Diggory following Sheridan.

"Bah, Bah so we're the sheep?"

"I guess that's up to you friend." Shepherd remarked evenly.

Sheridan felt their guide was familiar in a calming way. It was as if she had met him before. She hadn't seen him, but she knew about him in some way. She felt assured she'd remember during their journey.

Diggory didn't trust any of it. It would take much more for her young friend to get over years of anguish and drug induced paranoia. She could only imagine living on the streets, waiting for the next fix and hoping no one would kill you over a piece of cardboard box. He'd never defined that life, she could only try to imagine.

She sensed Diggory's trust in her, but knew trust was uncommon for him. *I must represent a motherly figure.*

They walked down Street to the path. Angel Choir strolled up the opposite side toward Angel Choir Chapel. "Shepherd, what can you tell me about Angel Choir? They never seem to notice us. I can barely hear them, but the hum of their chanting is beautiful. I'm especially impressed by their diversity considering their uniforms. All different, but not one challenges their position, they are very odd."

"Angel Choir isn't odd for them Sheridan. Have you ever seen a school where all the children wear uniforms?"

"Yes, but this can hardly be the same thing."

"No, it isn't the same thing, but they wear their uniforms without question much like children in school. Their purpose is to praise the king through song. They don't need to question what they love." Shepherd explained. "You see differences that they don't even know to notice exist."

Diggory broke in, "There is a big difference from school children. A lot of kids hate school."

Shepherd and Sheridan laughed, but Diggory hung back shuffling his feet.

Chapter 11: The Canyon

Sheridan's internal compass was usually right on, but not here. "Do you have a compass in case we get lost?"

"A compass would not work here. We don't need one. I know exactly where we are all the time." Shepherd answered.

Diggory looked at her, twirling his finger around his ear behind Shepherd's back. "Why?"

"You question my ability to stay on the right path Diggory?"

"Why won't a compass work here? What makes you so confidant you won't get us lost?"

Shepherd turned and looked at Diggory, then reached down and picked up a rock. Pulling a needle from his pocket Shepherd lay it in his palm. He held the needle a small distance from his hand and the needle immediately followed the piece of rock wherever he moved it. "That is why friend, there is a lot of magnetite found around here."

Shepherd smiled, putting the stone in his pocket with the needle, "thus my magnetic quality." He dramatically feigned charm by flourishing his hand and arm in a fluttering motion as he bowed at the waist.

Sheridan couldn't help smiling at Shepherd's whimsy.

"Well, it seems this place just bends to your magnetism as you want it to, considering the way the people in Hidden flock to you. Lead on Shepherd."

Diggory's mocking tone dripped with the distrust.

Shepherd smiled again at his companions, turned and continued to walk without saying anything more.

They walked through the same meadow as the previous day. Sheridan took in the contour of the land and the layout of the landscape. The land was mostly flat with plush bluegrass. The fruit and nut trees seemed to circle around it. The trees seemed to form a barrier. Their thick growth was like a forest. The meadow was clear of trees except for a few near the center that seemed to form a canopy.

Without thinking, Sheridan bent down and ran her hand through the grass studying it. It was so smooth and soft. Each blade seemed a perfect match to the other. Then she noticed the one thing

that nothing she knew could explain.
There wasn't a single weed disturbing
the smooth grass.

Sheridan thought it was an
impossible scene, considering the
obvious design that put trees and plants
together. It seemed that no matter how
often she visited the meadow, she would
never feel any less amazed by it.

It finally dawned on her that this
meadow and Shepherd were the
suppliers to Hidden. What the meadow
didn't provide, Shepherd must, such as
the sheep he'd brought with him when he
arrived at the inn.

Shepherd and Diggory stood silently
by and said nothing as she analyzed her
surroundings.

"Those sheep you had with you
when we first saw you," Sheridan began,
"were they for Cook to butcher?"

"Yes, they were the best sheep of the flock. Their meat will be very good."

Shepherd guided them to some flat rocks near the center of the clearing. The canopy of trees Sheridan noticed before stood a short distance from them. They saw empty bowls, baskets full of bread and the produce of the trees. "Sit." Shepherd motioned to three very clean stones surrounding the large, table rock.

"Wow," Sheridan interjected, "I certainly never noticed these stones before." Their guide left them and went to the lake. The two incidental companions watched Shepherd dip his hands in three times. With each dip, he pulled out a large salmon. He then pulled a knife from his pocket and cleaned them, washing them in the lake.

"What is this place?" They chimed together when he returned.

"Home," a single word reply, but why did it seem to answer the question, at least for Sheridan. She looked back at her life and wondered if she was destined to find Hidden all along.

She knew she was changing. Was she - home?

"How will you cook them? Diggory asked. This time his voice sounded curious.

"You see the rock in the middle? The sun is directly on that rock. Feel the heat coming from it, but don't touch it."

Shepherd waited for them to hold their hands over the rock. Sheridan and Diggory looked at each other astonished.

Shepherd wrapped each fish in a large leaf along with herbs, figs, and dates from the meadow and laid them on the rock. They could hear the fish cook inside the leaves. Sheridan's stomach growled as the smell of the cooking salmon filled the air. She giggled and then Diggory's stomach growled as if answering hers. The three laughed.

After their meal, they lounged in the grass under the canopy of trees.

Sheridan didn't remember falling asleep. When Diggory opened his eyes he looked confused.

Their guide was calling, "Come on you two, we need to continue our journey."

At the edge of the meadow, Shepherd turned to them. "From here we enter Dark Canyon. You must stay with me to be safe. I will not lead you the wrong way."

Diggory's eyes widened in fear, "Oh no. I've seen into that place. The smell alone is like something dead. I couldn't see much, but what I did sure didn't look healthy."

"Trust me." Shepherd said softly.

Sheridan climbed enough mountains and rocks to know they held many dangers. Taking the right trail and finding the right hand and footholds could be vital to survival. She decided to do exactly as their leader said.

She stepped forward and Diggory put a protective arm in front of her blocking her way.

"Dig?"

"I don't think I trust him that much yet."

Shepherd walked over and whispered something to Diggory that Sheridan couldn't hear. Without any more argument, the young man let his arm slide down and he took her elbow.

Sheridan didn't pull away. Her young friend was taking a leap forward to trust Shepherd, and Sheridan knew it had something to do with what Shepherd whispered into Diggory's ear.

Leaving the meadow, the air seemed filled with a sense of foreboding and the smells of rotting vegetation and death.

Shepherd picked up a long stick that he used to explore anything that looked dangerous, or shadowed in darkness. They could hear the sticks crunching under their feet. They felt odd to

Sheridan and she reached down and picked one up. She stopped and dropped it back on the ground.

"What was that?" Diggory asked.

"It was a human femur."

A creature jumped out of a bush as soon as Shepherd whacked a dying plant. It snarled at them with an almost human growl. The voice reminded her of the hiss of a cat, but it spat acid so strong it seared something in their path.

The creature was almost two feet tall with a badger like head. Its feet and hands resembled a human's except each digit twisted like those of a bramble bush. The beast's belly was sunken. It reached onto the ground grabbing a piece of skeletal remains and ate it like soft bread.

Sheridan's stomach turned over. She was so shaken Diggory grabbed her around the waist and steadied her. She could feel the young man shaking almost as much as she was.

"Back off Zaph, or you will kneel before me." Shepherd said with an emphasis on the word kneel.

"Never shall I bow to thee, Shepherd." The creature's high-pitched voice blew hot wind that felt like standing by a furnace.

"Evils like Zaph are the reason I don't want anyone walking this canyon without me." Shepherd told his two followers who moved a step closer to their guide. Zaph tried to grab Diggory's leg but Shepherd was quick to whack it back with his stick. The impish looking little monster growled, showing its pointed teeth.

"Shepherd, this is not anywhere near Nebraska is it? Have we died? Are you leading us through some hell cave?" Sheridan asked as the tears ran down her face. She wasn't crying. The stench of death made her eyes water.

"No, we are not in Nebraska." Shepherd moved closer putting a friendly arm around Sheridan's shoulder. "You are not dead and I am leading you out of this hellish canyon."

Sheridan wanted to stop, but it was out of the question. She didn't look back because she knew the awfulness that was there. Confused she continued to follow.

"What do you mean by that?" She whined.

"You must trust me."

"We have been," Diggory broke in agitated and moving closer to Sheridan as if to protect her from Shepherd. "You asked me back in the clearing to help you by trusting in you and helping Sheridan through this canyon. I'm not so sure I was smart to agree."

"Diggory, follow me and you will get your answers. I am protecting you both. These creatures can't harm you as long as I am with you. We will make it through. The bone you found, Sheridan, was from someone who thought they didn't need me. I am the guide who gets you through."

The idea of going forward without knowing what was ahead almost paralyzed the woman. Would he be able to protect them from all Evils on the journey? "Just take us back to Hidden." Sheridan pleaded.

"Sheridan," Shepherd soothed, "You have given me more trust than your friend, because of the trust Vida has in me. She would still ask that you trust me, even here."

"But, she's never been beyond the meadow. How can you be so sure?" Sheridan heard herself whining like a child. Clearing her throat, her voice deepened to a natural pitch. "Why would she trust you to take her into this dark canyon?"

"Because, Vida knows me well and has trusted me for a long time. She trusts me completely."

"I swear the two of you sound like lovers." Sheridan giggled scornfully.

Shepherd smiled. "We do love each other Sheridan. We love each other as lifelong friends love one another. I cannot take you back to Hidden. We must move on a little faster so we aren't caught in here after nightfall."

"Okay," Sheridan sighed and shook her head. "I will have to trust you. I can't do anything else."

Diggory's silence caused Sheridan to look up at her companion. He shrugged his shoulders.

As they continued on their way, they felt the crunching of charred bones, dead branches and fallen rocks under their feet.

Every few feet another acid spitting creature like Zaph would hiss as it shrank away from a mere glance from Shepherd. He obviously had a frightening authority over the Evils.

Sheridan was amazed at how fast her fright dissipated. With each encounter, it became more obvious they were under Shepherd's protection.

Diggory's grip on her loosened until both were walking beside each other, arms swinging.

It was odd, that lack of fear, especially under the circumstances. She felt she should at least be a little alarmed and ready for what might be ahead. "Yea, though I walk through the valley of the shadow of death, I will fear no evil."

"What was that?" Diggory asked. "Grandmother used to quote that to me all the time."

Before Sheridan answered, Shepherd continued. 'For thou art with me, Thy rod and thy staff they comfort me.' It is from Psalm 23 dear friend. It's a favorite with many."

"It seems to fit this place. I'm not afraid of the dark ugliness of it, not now anyway." Sheridan dropped her voice. "Did you feel it Dig? Did you feel the fear melt away?"

"I guess I kind of did, now that you mention it. Maybe it's because of our fearless leader."

Sheridan couldn't decipher Diggory's tone. He seemed sincere, but his attitude waxed hot and cold since she'd met him. He had lost so much in his young life. Her mother used to tell her that no matter how bad you think you have it, someone has it worse. She'd resented that idea, but now
she understood it.

"Woops, Sheridan you better come back to earth and watch your step." Diggory said as she stumbled over a root at her feet.

"Thank you, Dig." Her breathing quickened as she thought about what she could have fallen on.

"Shepherd, how can you walk through all this with bare feet? Don't the sharp rocks and rubbish cut your feet?"

"Don't worry about my feet, Sheridan; they are used to being exposed. You should be more concerned with watching where you step as Diggory said."

The rugged canyon was deep with sharp rock cliffs on each side. If not for the width, it would have been a crevice instead of a canyon. The darkness seemed to lighten as they walked and then close back in behind them. A glow emanated from Shepherd that Sheridan could only equate with an odd species of florescent fish in the deepest parts of the ocean.

"No way," Diggory exclaimed, "How did you do that?"

"Hello Az." Shepherd greeted someone or something. "These two aren't for you."

Sheridan felt a tap on her shoulder as Diggory drew her attention to a shadowy figure winging around the edge of the glow. It never attempted to come closer and Sheridan thought it must be able to exist only outside the light. "What is that Shepherd?" She pointed to the figure.

A very low, gurgling voice echoed back. "I know I don't take these. I just like to walk along beside you when I can, Shepherd. I don't often get the chance in my work. There are so many sad souls to carry."

Shepherd chuckled looking at Sheridan and Diggory. "There is no reason to fear Az. He doesn't have the bite or hate Evils do. He just does his work. He must have some time between souls today."

"I've been bringing a few through every wee bit, but a walk with you is always welcome." The shadow stopped moving above them. "I hear death's bells. I must answer the call of the bells." The shadowy figure disappeared.

"I don't think I want to meet Az alone." Sheridan whispered.

"Az carries souls to their destination." Shepherd chimed in, "He's not a fearful creature. He's a sad one."

"I assume you're talking about souls people are done with." Diggory growled at Shepherd. "This is more than weird. I'll be glad to be out of this canyon. I'm not comfortable knowing your friendly with a death shadow."

"Az isn't death; he is only the carrier of souls. He isn't like the Evils. They are fearful only to those who refuse to let me guide them." Shepherd didn't say anymore.

"That's the only answer you have for us?"

"I didn't hear a question. Are you asking me a question or making an accusation?"

"Okay, well then I'm asking you to explain all of this, from Hidden to wherever this path goes. Back there with that acid spitting thing, I would have said you are good. But just now with that creature floating in the shadows, I'm not sure. Which is it?"

"I would think you would be able to answer that by now, Diggory. I assure you, I am of the Good." Sheridan was amazed at Shepherd's calm. Why wasn't he angry, like she would be? Even if she partially agreed with Diggory, he was pushing Shepherd.

"That's an odd way to say it. But, I'm glad you're a good guy." Diggory mocked.

Sheridan nudged Diggory again whispering, "Dig, quit trying to agitate him. He's done nothing to put us in danger. And, I feel safe with him even in this ugly canyon with its terrifying things."

"Ah, we are at the end of the canyon my followers. Now we will go to the mountain." Shepherd announced. Sheridan wondered if he'd heard her.

The path became smoother as it led upward out of the canyon and its darkness. The three travelers walked easily up the grade without a single stone underfoot. The glow around Shepherd dissipated as the light of the sun lit their way.

Sheridan considered the path and its easy grade. She looked upward and they were nearly at the top of what she would have called a hill. They came to a clear spot with a nice flat area.

"I think we should spend the night here?" Shepherd announced.

"Now that, I have no argument with," Diggory stretched his arms out and swayed his back like releasing the stress on a twisted rubber band.

Sheridan broke into the tension. "Shepherd, just out of curiosity, how far is the mountain? This is a hill."

Shepherd looked at her with a softness that told her he knew she was not challenging him. "We've been climbing a slight grade even within the canyon, but you are right. This is a foothill. We will get to the mountain tomorrow."

There were flat rocks as in the meadow so they sat. It was amazing how comfortable they seemed for stone. Maybe it simply felt better than being on their feet after walking on bones and stones, Sheridan thought.

"Shepherd, how do you explain the fish back there? I don't understand catching Salmon in a lake like that. They generally come from the ocean and swim upstream in fresh water rivers to spawn right?" Diggory continued trying to trip up Shepherd.

"Normally"

"Is there something leading into that lake? It doesn't seem to have much of a current and it looks landlocked. I figured it was spring fed."

"It is spring fed and abundantly stocked with all kinds of fish."

"Do you mean we could pull out trout, catfish, salmon, or whatever out of that lake? I can't fathom that. It doesn't make sense. I mean, Salmon have to spawn don't they?"

"You limit life so much. Haven't you ever hoped for the impossible? With all you've experienced here, why would you doubt? Why don't you believe that I could put my hand into that lake and pull out an eel?" Shepherd spoke gently to Diggory.

"Now you're making a fool of me." Diggory turned to look at their female companion. "Sheridan, I think you should stay closer to me. This guy just came out of the loony bin."

"Diggory, you are so full of pain, you have lost faith. You believe that Catch is a sorcerer, but you don't believe I am capable of miracles?" Shepherd challenged Diggory for a change. "Take a look behind you." Shepherd commanded.

As they did, they saw three small tents surrounding a fire.

Sheridan felt safer than in her church. She knew Diggory would come to understand in time.

After a supper of wild rabbit, watercress from a stream nearby, and wild berries, they tucked away in their tents. "Sheridan," she heard the sweet male voice of Shepherd calling.

"Yes?"

"Sheridan, find me and find the treasure of the Lunis Flower."

"Where?"

"When," Shepherd replied.

"When?"

"As you found the light in the darkness, you will also find the Lunis Flower."

Sheridan sat up and opened the entrance to her tent. She saw Shepherd stoking the fire at least 15 feet away. She scratched at the flap on Diggory's tent.

"What?"

Diggory threw open the flap of his tent. "Oh, Sheridan it's you. I must have fallen asleep. I thought I heard my Grandmother yelling at me and scratching at my door." He paused for a moment. "Funny, she never scratched at my door. Anyway, what's up?"

"Did you hear that voice? I thought it was Shepherd whispering to me outside my tent, but he's way over there." She pointed to where Shepherd was stoking the fire.

"Maybe you fell asleep and dreamed it. I'm not surprised we would have weird dreams after that canyon."

"Perhaps," Sheridan didn't argue with him, but she knew what she'd heard.

Chapter 12: Serpent

"Sheridan, wake up." Diggory was reaching into her tent grabbing at her toes.

"Uhh? What? Diggory what do you want? I was sleeping."

"You were talking in your sleep loud enough to wake me in my own tent. I could only make out the words 'look' and 'dark.'"

"Oh sorry, I'll try not to talk in my sleep." She grumbled. "I never knew I talked in my sleep."

The next morning they all gathered on the hilltop and looked below them into the deep canyon. It seemed overshadowed by an outcropping of rock along the opposing ridge.

"Wow," Diggory said, "Sheridan look at that rainbow." His words echoed back.

"Awesome!" Sheridan said loudly and listened for the echo. They all laughed and Diggory pointed to a space between the overhanging rocks on the opposite side of the canyon near the horizon. A rainbow seemed to make its way from the horizon, over the outcrop and disappear into the canyon below.

"Oh my lord, that is worth all the ugliness we went through!" Sheridan felt her eyes tearing from the beauty of the heavenly vision.

"Why do you say that?" Shepherd asked.

"A rainbow is a promise of what's ahead and a goodbye to what's behind." She wiped a few tears from her eyes. My

mother used to say that to me all the
time.

"She was right." Shepherd
remarked.

Diggory said his name softly and
got a faint echo, and then he spoke
loudly and heard the stronger repeat.
"We know why I heard you last night."
Diggory broke in.

"What?" Sheridan asked.

"Remember," Diggory said, "I woke
you up because you were talking in your
sleep. I heard you all the way over into
my tent."

"You did? I don't remember any of
that."

"Oh, well of course not. You woke
me up scratching on my tent making all

kind of racket and you don't even remember me waking you up. What's fair about that?" Diggory feigned disappointment.

'Not a dern thang, but that's fine with me." Sheridan said in her best hillbilly holler imitation. The echo came back with the same fake hillbilly twang. All three of them had a good laugh.

"That was awful Sheridan." Diggory said.

"He's right too." Shepherd laughed as heartily as his followers did.

"Follow me," Shepherd called. They set off down a well-worn path that looked to circle downwards for a short distance and then curve upward.

"Is that where we're going?" For the first time, Diggory walked along beside

Shepherd instead of following grudgingly. He pointed toward a bluff at the top of a mountain.

Shepherd nodded, "Yes, we will climb up to that mountaintop, but I will not be taking you down the other side."

"Why?" Diggory asked.

"I have been there one time and it was more horrifying than anywhere else I've ever been. Consider that the canyon I led you through was mild by comparison. Once was enough."

"Is there something bad in the mountains that frighten you?" Sheridan listened in as the two spoke.

"Within those mountains are many things. I went beyond them and had to battle my way back against Evils much, much worse than the ones we met in the canyon. I have no need to go that way again and neither do you."

"You mean you don't want us to go there."

Shepherd stopped on the path and turned to Diggory.

"I say what I mean, but you don't listen. Open up and hear." Shepherd admonished.

"Diggory," Sheridan growled softly as she tugged on his sleeve, "he is right. I understand him just fine. You need to open up to what he's saying to you."

"Why do you trust him? You had your own misgivings when we started into the canyon. You're buying into whatever this guy is selling."

"I know more now because I listen. There is nothing to buy into, Dig. I'm just accepting what he says. Shepherd hasn't led us into any danger. He's led us past it. I quit questioning him and started trusting when I saw his light in that canyon."

"What do you call that canyon? You're saying that wasn't dangerous. That acid spitting thing sure looked dangerous. Geez Sher, you are naïve."

"Maybe, but I didn't say the danger's weren't there, just that he never allowed them to hurt us. Have you forgotten so fast his glow that led us through that terrible place?"

"No, I remember that. I think he had a high power flashlight."

"One that has no dark spots and that gives a spherical light. Come on

239

Diggory, you are trying too hard for explanations."

"I don't get it. You are the scientist here Sher, and yet you are telling me to just accept all of this, and him, without questioning it. What gives?"

"I am a scientist, but I also know that many things are not explained away by the wisdom of science. Looking at science as the only answer to everything is a mistake that closes us off to the beauty of discovering things we can't explain away by it. That's what I tell my students. We can't discover the impossible if we look only for the possible."

"You're not like any science teacher I've ever had." Diggory sounded exasperated.

"Then you had the worst kind of science teachers." Sheridan was angry with Diggory now. She had been sad for him in Hidden, happy for him when his sores healed at the lake, afraid for him in the canyon, and now she was angry.

"Look at it like this. We once knew that things just fell, but we didn't care why. We knew the earth was flat. We knew the earth was the center of the universe. We knew people who got diseases were sinners." Sheridan spoke to Diggory more calmly hoping he would listen more to her calm than her unfortunate anger.

"Okay, but you are making an argument both for and against science Sher."

"Exactly," Sheridan replied.

"She is correct, Diggory." Shepherd spoke up as if he'd been listening to their entire conversation.

"You heard that, Shepherd?" Diggory said as if accusing the leader of eavesdropping.

"I couldn't really help it. Sheridan's embrace of principles for the tangible and intangible are refreshing. She understands a lot that you haven't, simply because she has experienced things you have not. She's learned to accept the unexplainable."

Diggory had a puzzled look on his face, but didn't say anymore. They walked in silence for a few minutes.

A bright vista of color spread out in front of them as they came over the top of the hill.

"Shep, I thought you said this was unforgiving territory. This place isn't bad at all."

"As long as I am with you, you can come to no harm. This spot can become temptation if you aren't careful. It sure looks better from up here." Shepherd smiled taking a deep breath.

"You sound like the Lord himself." Diggory chuckled at Shepherd.

"I am."
"Yeah, right," Diggory laughed as he once again looked at Sheridan and twirled his finger around his ear. Sheridan was crying for Diggory.

"Sheridan, don't fall for all this crap." Diggory sounded concerned.

"Diggory, I'm not the one falling right now."

As they descended below the jut of a rocky overhang, the sun's light dimmed.

Sheridan heard a noise in the leaf litter and debris on the path. She looked and saw a kind of snake she'd never seen before slithering up behind Shepherd.

"Watch out." She warned but it was too late, it had bitten his heel.

They couldn't see Shepherd's face but he didn't miss a step. He placed his heel down and the snakes head squeezed into the dirt of the path.

"Are you okay," They asked in unison.

"I'm okay, just a small bruise. I dare say he's going to have a headache. He won't be trying to bite you -not now."

"What about other snakes? There are bound to be more like him around here."

"Serpent, no he is a one of a kind Evil. He's older than the Earth."

"Nice metaphor," Diggory remarked.

"No, I don't' think that was a metaphor, Diggory."

"Okay, so I don't have your education, but I could have sworn metaphor was the correct word."

Sheridan shook her head. She'd hoped Diggory was getting closer to understanding what she'd discovered, but he wasn't quite there yet.

"What about your foot?" This time Diggory seemed concerned for their guide's safety.

"I'll take care of it."

"Physician heal thyself?"

Sheridan thought Diggory didn't sound mocking as before.

"Did your grandmother take you to church very often?" Shepherd asked Diggory.

"Why do I think you already know the answer?" Diggory looked at Sheridan with tears in his eyes.

"Diggory, I didn't tell him anything." Sheridan answered his unasked question. "No," Diggory wiped his face roughly with his sleeve. "then how does he know about my grandmother, church and everything else?"

"Diggory, we've been together the whole time except when we slept. When would I have told him anything? Besides, it was just a question. It wasn't a request for your life story."

Shepherd broke in. "Sheridan hasn't given me any information. I am simply curious because of your reference to a Bible verse."

"Okay, Yes, but I'm afraid I fell far away from where I began. I ended up cold and alone on the streets. Then a friend gave me the keys to a car and asked me to drive it to his mother's house across state. That's where I was headed." The young man got very quiet. He looked to Sheridan as if he had no way to complete his story.

The three stood on the barely worn path in tense silence as Diggory sank slowly to a sitting position on the ground. He cried as if every bit of the pain he'd faced in life was boiling over. Sheridan saw a man in front of her releasing years of pain from his spirit.

Then Diggory started to talk. He talked about the death of his parents. He'd felt abandoned after they died. He spoke of how his grandmother took him in and taught him.

Diggory spoke of many things, but mostly he confessed how he let his parents and grandmother down when he started using drugs to dull the pain. "I don't deserve anything good, they deserved it. My family raised me with love and taught me right from wrong. I had a ticket to a good life
and I blew it because I felt sorry for myself for losing all of them."

Diggory finally wore himself out and sat there wiping away the last of his tears. He'd finished crying and seemed embarrassed about it.

"Diggory, you take on too much. I've watched you all your life. I don't remember anything you did that placed a guilty verdict on your head." Shepherd announced.

"What? You are confusing me. There is no way you've watched me all my life, unless you're God or something." Diggory scoffed.

"It will come to you son, very soon."

"Listen to him Diggory. He is the teacher here."

"I believe that. He does a lot of teaching. I'm even beginning to accept some of it." Diggory sounded tormented. "But, come on Sher. Even you can't fall for that "known you all your life crap."

Sheridan hooked her arm in Diggory's as if she was helping him for a change. "Come on, we don't have to talk about that now. I'm not sure what Shepherd meant by that, but I think it's time you got up off the ground and stood tall." Sheridan tugged on his arm.

Diggory stood up and smiled. From then he seemed to walk with more bounce in his step as if he weighed less.

Chapter 13: Journey to the Mountain

The mountain was not so difficult to climb as Sheridan expected. In fact, they needed no gear at all. They were following a grown over but worn path slowly up the side of the mountain. The incline was steep, but not treacherous. Shepherd tended to take the lead a few feet ahead, but

Sheridan was convinced he was very aware of everything they said and did. The way he would break into their conversations at opportune times suggested he listened intently.

"How tall is this mountain?" Sheridan asked.

"Oh it's a little over three thousand feet from the base." Shepherd answered.

"What do you think about following Shep up the mountain?" Diggory asked Sheridan.

"What about it Dig?" Sheridan asked again.

"If he's a teaching Shepherd, what do you suppose he is going to teach us at the top?" Diggory said imitating some television actor that Sheridan couldn't put a name to.

"I think Shepherd is the teacher and I'll let him instruct."

"Okay, Teach, before we go any further, how can we be sure that what you have up there won't kill us? We've come across some terrible stuff on the way." Diggory taunted Shepherd.

"I don't know what more I can do to convince you Diggory. I haven't let anything harm you yet have I?"

"No, but where did you come from?"

"Father," Shepherd answered.

"Oh, that's easy, we all have fathers. Give me a break and answer my question."

"I did. I come from my father."

"Okay, I'll bite." Diggory said. "Who is your father?"

"My Father is the King of Good."

"What? If that's true, why are you out here stumbling over sharp rocks in bare feet, being bitten by a snake, and herding sheep?" Diggory almost sounded triumphant.

"It won't be much farther." Was all Shepherd would say.

"Can we sit and talk for a bit?" This time Sheridan spoke up.

"Sure?" Shepherd stopped and turned around to look down at them.

"I'm beginning to have more questions now. I have been following you and more and more I feel a connection. But, I'm wondering if it's a true connection or is it something I only hope for? I'm a little frightened at what may be at the top of this mountain." Sheridan felt like a small child.

"You are an interesting pair." Shepherd remarked almost as if he was speaking about them instead of too them.

"Why do you say that?" Sheridan could understand why one would say that, but what was Shepherd's point?

"Why do you think I chose the two of you to be together on this journey?" Shepherd asked.

"You chose us? I don't get it." The question puzzled Sheridan "You had no one else to bring. It was only the two of us."

"How did you get to Hidden?" Shepherd kept asking odd questions.

"I was on my way to a book signing and the fog forced me off the road. I ended up in Hidden. I haven't been able to get back out." Sheridan answered "But, you knew that didn't you?"

"And you Diggory, how did you find yourself in Hidden?"

"I was driving a car across country to its owner to make some money. I was in a gas station and some guys came in and caused some trouble. I high tailed it out of there, but I haven't the foggiest idea how I got to Hidden." Diggory expounded.

"Okay, now I will explain part of what is happening to you." Shepherd announced. "Sheridan, you were not able to pull out of the fog because your car flipped over and you were thrown out of it. You are in a coma."

Sheridan's shock was obvious. "You are lying to me, Shepherd. I put trust in you." Sheridan was crying.

"The phone call you made to your family, was it odd that they said it was okay and they were waiting for you?"

"I didn't think so at the time." Sheridan replied.

"After all that time of not being able to call anyone outside of Hidden, you find yourself in a replica of your home, making a call to your family. That wasn't odd to you?"

"Well, yes that was very odd."
Sheridan's voice quivered.

"Talking to your family was real,
but you weren't on a phone. You're
house was some of Catch's sorcery. He'd
been trying to pull you to his side before
I returned."

"Why would Catch deceive me like
that?" Sheridan asked. "How could he
put my home there in such a short time?
Nobody seems to have an answer for
that except sorcery."
"He is a sorcerer of the worst kind.
He is a deceiver. He conjured much in
your mind."

"Okay," Diggory chimed in. "What
is all this? If he is an evil sorcerer, what
are you? Why are you upsetting
Sheridan so much if Catch is the bad
one?"

"This is a place my father chose. Armies of followers built it. Catch didn't like that and so he sent his Serpent to destroy it. We didn't let him destroy the meadow. Father banned Catch because of his evil destruction. This was once a beautiful place. Now it's a dark canyons and a rocky mountainside." If there was a way of being calmly passionate, Shepherd's composure as he spoke would fit that description.

"Wait. I'm totally lost. Why are Sheridan and I an odd pair?" Diggory broke in.

"You are a drug addict who has been lost, but your roots are good. Those men you saw blew up that gas station. They were not there for money. They were there to destroy. When you tried to leave, they shot the gas pumps and your car caught fire and exploded.

Diggory exploded, "You liar."

"No Diggory, it's not a lie."
Shepherd spoke softly.

Shepherd motioned for them to sit
on a rocky ridge not far from the path.
Their legs hung over the canyon below.
Shepherd remained just above them on
the path.

"Do you feel safe sitting there?"

"Well, yes, as long as nobody
pushes us off." Sheridan replied and
Diggory nodded.

"There was a time my Father asked
me to trust that he would not let me fall.
I slid to the very edge. Catch was with us
and wanted to test my father because he
wanted to make me doubt the King.
Catch pushed me and as I was at the
precipice falling over the edge when at

once my father was immediately before me." With that statement, Shepherd was face to face with Sheridan and Diggory.

Sheridan gasped and looked down to see what Shepherd was standing on, but his feet were not touching anything. He was in mid-air.

Shepherd continued, "Father pushed me back on the ledge and held me up. It was that day that he banished Catch from his kingdom. He said that Catch had many chances to quit challenging him, but he continued to rebel."

As Shepherd spoke, he moved in the air to stand on the edge of the rock ledge where Sheridan sat with Diggory. The two followers immediately stood up and placed their backs to the mountainside's wall.

"If Catch knew your father would banish him, why did he keep doing things to make him mad?" Sheridan was breathing heavily in awe of what she'd just witnessed. Her hand to her chest, she felt something jump inside her and knew she was alive as never before.

"Jealousy, he wanted to take my father's power. Catch wanted my father's kingdom, but now he wants to destroy it and make his own kingdom here." Shepherd stretched his arms out indicating the expanse of all the places they had been.

"Except for the meadow, which I call the garden, Catch wants it all. The meadow is mine, and I will not allow him there." The Shepherd reached down and dusted off his feet with his hands. Sheridan wasn't sure why he would do that.

"Enough of that, Catch can no longer take either of you."

"So, none of this is real?" Sheridan asked. "This is all a dream I'm having in a coma?"

"I want to know too, Shepherd. I-I believe you, but what is real? You have led me through all of this, or I've dreamed it? What is real?"

"You are both real. This place is real. Just because you are in a coma, doesn't mean you are not with me now, or that you are not both real. You are both here with me making this journey so that you can know me more completely. Think of it as an in between" Shepherd explained. "Hidden is the entrance to this place. You are prepared in Hidden. Catch knew he could not have your souls because they already belonged to me from when you first believed as children."

"Give me a minute to absorb this." Sheridan said. She took and deep breath and felt like the earth below her feet moved. She was dizzy and felt much like she did in Hidden that first day when she tried to cross Street. She sat back on the rock ledge.

"I believe you, Shepherd. What you have said explains so much about the past few days. If this is real and yet we are there, what about our bodies here?" Sheridan asked.

"Your earthly bodies are still in those hospital beds. You are also real here. These bodies are your real bodies here, but they are not sick. You were healed at the lake, but only in these bodies. You are in between your life on earth, and your life that will be forever."

"Oh, Dear Lord" Diggory slumped down on his knees. You are THE Lord Prince."

Sheridan also bowed down on her knees on the rock ledge. "Lord Prince, I have known, but I still doubted you. Please forgive me."

"Get up, both of you." Shepherd held his hands out for them both. "You have been forgiven. Don't you know that I love you? You are my brother and sister, my friends, and so much more. I've waited for you because I love you both." He folded both of them into his arms.

"I'm still confused, Shepherd, I mean Lord Prince." Diggory spoke as if he was in terrible pain. His eyes turned down to the ground. "You heard me earlier talking about all the terrible things I've done to support my addictions." Diggory's loud cry as he slid to a fetal position sounded so full of pain, Sheridan wanted to run to him.

Shepherd sat down beside the young man. If Shepherd had any judgment toward Diggory, Sheridan could not see it in anything Shepherd said or did.

"Oh, well that explains it." Shepherd spoke softly. "If you spoke of it in a way that was remorseful and seeking forgiveness, I would not remember it at all and neither will the King." Shepherd sat with his arm around Diggory's shoulder as the young man cried out years of torment.

Sheridan looked at her young friend as if he was someone new. She had watched the rebirth of his spirit. His smile softly grew through the tears. His

eyes darted as if they were seeing
everything new.

"Diggory, how wonderful,"
Sheridan hugged her friend closely.

"Let's move on up the mountain."
Shepherd spoke with a quiet authority
that Sheridan knew and understood.

Chapter 14: Top of the Mountain

As they reached the summit of the mountain, they could see a tree with a strong straight trunk and large broken branch nailed and strapped with leather lashings to hold it in a cross position. The top of the tree was blooming with beautiful yellow flowers.

Diggory walked to a piece of rock that stood slightly higher than the rest of the mountain. It looked like a very shallow cave. To one side was a large boulder. When the other two caught up to him, Diggory pointed out a large rut in the ground where the bolder must have slid in front of the opening.

"Oh, my dear Lord," Sheridan exclaimed as she thought of what occurred on that mountain. "You paid it all didn't you?"

He held out his hands palms up and as he pulled up his sleeve, they saw scars at the base of each where it met the wrist.

"Stand up, you are free." Shepherd announced.

"You are my diamonds, perfected by our love. I'd do it again to help you shine like diamonds and rubies against the sun."

Shepherd's voice sounded soft and almost prayerful. "Look over the edge of the cliff past those rocks."

They did as he instructed and looked into a pit so black they had no idea where it ended. They could hear horrible screeches coming from that chasm.

Sheridan felt something on her ankle. When she looked down a small hand grasped her ankle and a larger hand grasped Diggory's. "Catch," Sheridan whispered.

"Be gone." Shepherd's voice sounded like roll of thunder. Immediately the hands released the two and disappeared. An angry roar bellowed up along with a stench of volcanic sulfur.

"Where is the other side?" Sheridan jumped back from the edge. "Where is the other side?" She was pointing across the blackness of the chasm into a blacker void. It was as if they were at the edge of the earth.

"There is no other side." Shepherd replied. "This is one destination that is forever, but it is not for you or Diggory."

"That is where you went to fight that terrible battle. I remember reading about it now. The Book said you fought and came back." Diggory held his nose as if an unbearable odor overcame him. "That sulfur is making me feel ill."

"Yes, and you have no need to go there" Shepherd remarked. "That place is for those who would not listen or believe. They insisted they didn't need or want me or my father." The Shepherd was weeping. The tears flowed over the edge and the sizzle of steam reached them like pouring water over hot coals.

Sheridan and Diggory sniffed the air.

"The air is clean again." Sheridan as she took a deep breath. She looked at Shepherd with new understanding of the love Service and Cook held in their hearts for Shepherd.

"Let us leave this place. We will never return here." Shepherd commanded.

Sheridan smiled and looked up at Shepherd. "I still haven't seen the Lunis Flower. Will we go find that now?"

Shepherd smiled, but didn't answer.

Chapter 15: Haven

Shepherd waved his arm and instantly they were in the meadow.

Diggory laughed. "Wow,I didn't feel anything, we just turned up here. How, oh never mind." He smiled and Sheridan knew he finally knew the power of the Shepherd's presence.

Sheridan didn't hear any challenge in his voice.

"Why didn't I feel you in my life? After grandma died and they took the house and all, I had nothing left". Diggory's voice was sharper now, his breathing faster.

"I never left you. You put up barriers. I was still there. When you let the world in, you listened to people who didn't care about you, you couldn't find me, because that world was in the way."

"Why is there so much anger and hate in the world? Why are so many starving? I only" Diggory spoke softly. "I only ask because it is a question the world has never answered. They blame you for all the bad things that happen."

"My lambs, not everything that happens in the world is by My Father's bidding or mine. Many things that happen are not because of any judgment. We created you, but you have always had free will. People have populated the earth and mingled. Once cast out of the garden, humans were susceptible to disaster and disease. They simply didn't have the protection of the Garden anymore."

"You mean there were bad things in the world then?" Sheridan asked. "I learned that God created everything right? He created a perfect world with perfect humans."

"Yes that is true. Things such as bacteria aren't meant to be bad. In fact, they do many good things. But, the treatment of the perfect by imperfect beings tainted them and made them harmful. Even the Serpent was a perfect being before he challenged God."

Sheridan knew who Shepherd was, and she could see that Diggory also knew Him. The two sat at the feet of the Shepherd listening to every word. When the time came for them to move on and Shepherd motioned for them to get up.

"We are too far aren't we?" Sheridan asked.

Shepherd laughed and motioned them on. "You are like my disciples were. They still questioned my words when they knew who I was. You will see. In the canyon, you saw the light and I guided you with it."

"Kind of like the wise men."
Diggory chuckled.

Shepherd laughed with them as if they were sharing a wonderful joke.

"What about the Tree of Knowledge in the Garden of Eden?" Sheridan asked. "Which fruit did they eat? People have been trying to figure that out forever."

"People are either too literal or too analytical. The kind of fruit they ate wasn't the problem. The tree was the Tree of the Knowledge of Good and Evil because evil dwelled in it. Do you remember who was in the tree?"

"The serpent was in the tree," Diggory answered.

"Exactly, it was the only place he could get into the Garden. He was so beautiful and full of charisma. Still can be, but he's always challenging us. Father forbade the serpent to come into the Garden. So he climbed into that tree and hid there. The warning Father gave to Adam and Eve to stay away from the tree had little to do with the fruit. The warning was to guard man's innocence and keep him away from the serpent."

A loud gasp escaped Sheridan. "Catch, back at the inn, catch wanted me visit his garden from the inn. What kind of garden could Catch have?

"A garden of death." Four words from Shepherd revealed Catch as the serpent, and all else evil.

"I understand that," Diggory said as if surprised that he did. "How long have I been in the coma?"

"A few hours," Shepherd replied.

"I thought I'd been here for several days. So Catch was telling the truth when he said this was a different realm and time was not what it seemed."

"He's quite capable of telling the truth when it serves him. Partial truths are his best weapon." Shepherd answered.

Diggory bowed and kissed Shepherd's hand. "I will never question your love for me again."

"I know son."

They walked back toward Hidden. "That sign," Sheridan pointed in shock.

"It says Welcome to Haven. What happened to Hidden?"

"Look," Shepherd pointed across Street as they stepped onto the walk on the Heaven's Choir side of the street.

"Oh," Sheridan waved at Cook and Service who were standing outside the café with three young people.

"They can't hear you Sheridan. They are preparing a new flock."

Sheridan and Diggory looked at each other. Heaven's Choir was walking toward them singing loudly, "Halleluiah, God the Father. Halleluiah God the risen Son, Halleluiah God the Spirit, Halleluiah God in Three."

"It is so...so... what can I call such music far beyond the beautiful melodies we used to sing in church? There is no comparison." Sheridan's face shone in a halo of light that filtered onto her from Shepherd.

Diggory pointed to her, and Sheridan pointed to Diggory for he looked fresh in new light, as she must. "We have arrived." Shepherd announced as he opened the Angel Choir Chapel.

"Diggory, this is where you go back. You're work begins now."

"What? No please Lord, don't make me go back to that life. I want to go with you, PLEASE."

Sheridan saw the pain of abandonment she'd watched him overcome.

"My son, you will not be going back to the same life you were living. I have other plans for you. Why do you think I would take you through the pathof so much darkness. You don't need that path if you were going with me to heaven now."

"Lord, don't desert me."

"Diggory, this is a privilege for you. You have the ability to go back from death and tell others of what you saw. What you lived here."

"They won't believe me."

"A lot of them won't. That's the way the world is, but I only need a few to believe you. They will go on to help others. Ultimately, the choice is yours. I want you to go back and lead others. But, all you have to do is not wake up."

Shepherd opened the gate to Heaven. "How many go in today?"

He held out his hands, palms up and motioned Sheridan in. Diggory didn't follow.

There were no questions for her to ask about it. She knew the answers inside the gate; inside the beautiful gardens of Heaven.

She sat on a marble bench covered with pure white pillows stitched with silver and gold thread.

Shepherd's robes changed to pure white. They had the glow of thousands of stars. However, they didn't hurt her eyes to look at. His head had a crown.

He pulled up his sleeve to reveal his scars. Then, the most amazing thing happened. A Lunis Flower grew up and opened into a bloom. It grew out of the scar on his wrist.

Sheridan drew in a breath, "Oh my dear Lord Jesus, you are so beautiful."

He held his wrist closer. "Pluck it from my wrist",

"Won't that hurt?"

"Sheridan this is heaven," Jesus chuckled.

She reached out and snapped the crisp fresh stem from below the the base of Jesus hand toward his arm.

"Pull off a leaf."

Sheridan pulled off one heart shaped leaf and looked up at him.

"Eat it."

She put the leaf in her mouth and instantly tasted blood and flesh. As she looked up again, Shepherd pulled off one white petal, and motioned her to do the same.

The golden colored seeds of the stamen turned to gleaming gold. She felt a finedust falling all around the crown of her head.

She looked down and saw that she was wearing a white silk gown.

Her Savior from Hidden, Shepherd, joined in the song of Heaven's Choir.

Sheridan sang out with a pure voice of perfect pitch and tone.

"Oh, my Lord," She looked at the man she'd known as Shepherd and now as Jesus her Savior, "I know the word on the plaque outside my room at Hide Inn.

It's my new name. I am Naomi." She
paused. "I am Naomi."

"You are not in Hidden anymore
Naomi." Jesus Christ proclaimed.
"Amen, it is everlasting." Jesus raised
his arms high and then took Naomi's
hands.

Epilog

Diggory heard the buzz of machines around him. "Jesus? Sheridan?"

He thought he was speaking aloud but something was in his throat, and between his teeth. Opening his eyes, Diggory could see machines with tubes, though his vision was foggy.

"Your awake! Let me get this tube out of your throat, and we'll see how well you do breathing without the machine."

Diggory gagged and felt nauseated producing a raspy caugh as the nurse tugged the tube until it cleared his throat.

"Take in slow easy breaths. Your throat will be sore for a while."

Tears well up, "Jesus, Sheridan, where are they?"

"Well last I heard Jesus is in heaven and I don't know any Sheridan that isn't a patient. Do you have a friend or family member named Jesus or Sheridan?"

"In the meadow...She's in Heaven."

"Sir, you've been in a coma. You must have had some great dreams."

A woman about 35 knocked on the door of the room. Alarms weregoing off from somewhere close enough to hear, but they soundedlike they were through a wall.

The nurse raised Diggory's head in the hospital bed. He saw the woman looking at him. "Sheridan?" He pointed to her and grabbed the nurse's arm.

"Nurse," The other woman with red hair spoke. "I think my sister is gone."

"That Sheridan!" Diggory coughed the name as he pointed at a woman just outside hide door.

"What?" The woman from just outside his door went pale. The near mirror image of Sheridan looked at Diggory.

"My sister's name is Sheridan. Do you know her?"

"She was with me. In the meadow with Shepherd, I mean" He produced a harsh cough and continued. "Jesus."

"Oh, dear Lord." The woman rushed to Diggory's bedside. "You saw her?

She tried to hug him but the nurse held a hand out to stop her. Diggory's burns on his legs and torso were mostly stage 3. The blisters from the stage 2 burns broke easily.

"I'm sorry. I almost hurt you. I just lost my sister. She's been in a coma too."

"Sheridan is with Jesus." Diggory's eyes filled with tears. "I want be with her."

His breathing became labored, body jolting as he coughed.
"I think you'd better go Dear," He's wearing down.

"Thank you, I believe you."
Sheridan's sister smiled as she left his room crying.

*****

Five years had passed since Diggory's recovery. His mind was as clear about Hidden, Shepherd and Sheridan as ever.

"Pastor?" a woman knocked at his door.

"Yes, Mrs. Wilson, lets go into the sanctuary since there is nobody else here today, except Mrs. Nash." Diggory looked at his dedicated if elderly secretary. "Mrs. Nash, please see that we are not interrupted."

The woman's husband died the week before. Diggory had a unique gift helping people dealing with loss.